Kittyzen's Arrest

Country Cottage Mystery #1

Addison Moore

and

Bellamy Bloom

Books by the Authors

1

My name is Bizzy Baker, and I can read minds. Not every mind, not every time—but it happens, and believe me when I say it's not all it's cracked up to be.

"Good morning." I hold up the carafe to the elderly man reading his paper. As the manager of the Country Cottage Inn, I certainly don't mind helping out in the café when it's needed. "More coffee?"

"Please." He nods politely. ***Lovely lady. Lovely inn. I'm glad I talked my wife into coming here.*** He frowns a moment. ***Fine. She talked me into it. As she likes to remind me, she's always right. I'll never admit to it, but it sure is true.***

I can't help but chuckle as I fill his mug to the brim. Reading minds isn't always this pleasant. For instance, the time I was at junior prom and my date smiled right at me and thought to himself how much the dress I was wearing belonged on a corpse at the morgue. Or the time I shared my first kiss, and the boy whose lips had just assaulted mine brazenly wished I was some girl named Tina.

I'm not Tina. I will never be Tina, but at times I've wished I could trade places with just about anyone.

My name is *Bizzy*, and I'm a twenty-six-year-old woman who has ended up as the manager of the Country Cottage Inn, right here in Cider Cove, Maine, where I grew up.

I head to the next table, to a girl with her hair up in a messy bun, books strewn across the table, glasses slung low on her nose, and she happens to have a Dexter University sweatshirt on. I hold up the carafe and she signals for me to proceed.

I'm going to need all the free refills I can get. She looks down and frowns at her books. *Who am I kidding? There's not enough coffee in the world to help me get through this semester. The mechanics and special relativity of physics? What was I thinking signing up for that class? I'm really in over my head this time.*

I point down to her physics book and smile. "You've got this. Just take lots of notes and read everything they assign."

Common sense wins again. The girl looks momentarily relieved. "Thank you. That actually does make me feel a bit better."

I give a little wink before heading to the back of the café.

Ah, Dexter University. I've only left Cider Cove once and that was to attend Dexter where I nearly completed my undergraduate work—and by nearly, I mean I was one semester shy of earning that shiny new degree, but like most things in life I was terrified of reaching that goal. And trust me, I don't like the fact I hightailed it right back to Cider Cove with my scholastic tail between my legs as an official college dropout, but the more I thought about the pressure graduation would bring, the more I was convinced I couldn't do it.

A brunette with long dark curls hovers over her phone and I stop cold in my tracks.

My goodness, is that Mack? The girl looks up briefly, and thankfully it's not her.

"More coffee?" I ask as I breathe a sigh of relief.

"Yes, and keep it coming."

"Not a problem." I quickly refill her mug, but I can't seem to pick up on any thoughts she's having. Some people are simply impossible to read and I have no idea why.

Mack comes to mind once again.

The entire mind reading debacle can be traced back to that fateful Halloween party I attended when I was thirteen with my very best friends, Emmie Crosby and Mackenzie—*Mack* Woods. Let's just say an innocent game of bobbing for apples went horrifically wrong.

Emmie was nowhere to be found. Come to find out, she had cornered her junior high crush at the pumpkin carving station and there were both sharp knives and first kisses involved.

But Mack and I were going for the apple bobbing gold—or so I thought. Let's just say Mack's efforts to help me secure my mouth over a juicy red apple were less successful in that arena than they were in her efforts to send me to the other side of existence.

The more I struggled to come up for air, the more Mack would hold me under, seemingly cheering me on until she finally pushed me right into the giant whiskey barrel that housed the slippery fruit.

I hit the bottom of the barrel headfirst so hard I saw stars right there under water. It was a nightmare of splashing and twisting and turning, and no matter how hard I tried, I couldn't seem to untangle my limbs and stand up.

Four things came from that horrific nightmare. One: I have an irrational fear of large bodies of water. Confession: I haven't swum since the incident and don't plan to anytime in the future. Just the thought of the water engulfing me and my inability to breathe or reach the surface scares the living daylights out of me. But since living in coastal Maine makes it nearly impossible to avoid the water, I've adopted a rule I can live with. As long as the water never goes higher than my ankles, I'm fine with walking the shoreline.

Two: I'm terrified of confined spaces. I suspect tumbling around in a dark whiskey barrel filled with water will do that to a person.

Three: It initiated my distrust of Mack Woods.

Mack and I grew up together.

Mack, Emmie, and I used to be an unbreakable trio—that is, right up until high school when Mack saw fit to steal every boy that I even remotely showed any interest in.

And after she went home with my date at prom, I decided it was time to cut ties, and thankfully Emmie sided with me. I don't know what I would have done if I had lost Emmie's friendship, too. Although, I've never counted it a loss to be rid of Mack.

And last but not least, number four: It was from that day on that I suddenly had the ability to pry into other people's minds. And, believe me, I did not like what I heard. Apparently, Mack has never had a high opinion of me, but words like *suffering* and *pity* were used when she was seemingly forced to be in my presence. And forced by who?

I have no idea, but she was never without a fake smile and a mean thought thereafter.

And let's just say listening in on other people's thoughts hasn't been a picnic either. Suffice it to say, I don't bother asking people how my outfit looks, or what they think of my new haircut.

On the surface, everyone is exceedingly polite, but peel back the curtains and you get a lot of truth you didn't bargain for. And that includes my mother and my sister Macy, too. Of course, they weren't having cruel thoughts about me, just exceptionally honest ones. The only person who has never had so much as a criticism of me has been Emmie. Every thought that girl has about any and everyone is one hundred percent pure.

In fact, I've become so wrapped up in people's honest criticisms, I've created an entire list of my own to go along with them. And for good reason. No matter how hard I seem to want something, it seems the farther away it gets. Take for instance the fact I love to bake. Well, if I don't burn it, I find something else that will botch up the recipe. Thankfully, Emmie is an excellent baker and gladly takes my ideas and runs with them. She's so sweet to me, she tries to give me credit for her yummy desserts, but I would never dream of letting people think I had a hand in making them.

And that leads me back to why I dropped out of college. Since I was little, the one thing I wanted more than anything was to run my own business. My mother had her own realty company at the time and I wanted to be just like Mom, a large-and-in-charge success, holding the world by her purse strings. But since I seemed to burn everything in the kitchen—and burn down all the good things I touched in general, I decided to run from my collegiate endeavor as well.

Instead of finishing college, I hightailed it right back to this sleepy seaside town, Cider Cove.

I set down the carafe and head outside of the café right past the patio and onto the white sandy beach where my cat springs up out of nowhere.

I sigh dreamily as the sapphire waves crash over the shoreline. My sweet kitten, whom I aptly and ironically named *Fish*, and I stride farther away from the Cottage Café and watch as the morning swells foam over the shoreline. Fish is a four-month-old black and white longhaired tabby that I found mewling her poor little heart out behind my sister's soap and candle shop, Lather and Light, just up the way on Main Street. I took the poor little thing straight to the vet, and once it was determined she was a stray, I took her into my home and my heart.

"Let's walk out farther," I say as Fish threads in and around my ankles. Fish doesn't seem to mind the sand. In fact, she finds it amusing if anything. Since Fish is so good with people, I have her with me at all times while I'm at work. She loves the inn and she loves the pets that come through it as well.

To the water's edge! she cries out—of course, it's all in her mind. We've been communicating this way since I brought her home and we're both quite happy with the situation. I can't hear every animal's thoughts, but it's few and far between when I don't.

"Careful," I call out after her. "You know how we both feel about water."

I'll never touch the stuff. There's not a beast on the planet that will ever make me dip a paw into it.

A dry laugh pumps from me as I glance back at the inn. It's a tall and stately structure with a stone façade, blue shutters over the windows, and ivy covering its every free surface.

The Country Cottage Inn isn't only a rather large hotel set right on the beach, but it boasts of over three dozen cottages that we rent out that extend over the rolling hills behind the inn itself. I reside in one, as does my best friend Emmie. Her brother lives in another, and my Grandma, who is technically nobody's grandmother, lives in the cottage just beyond the main entry.

In fact, the Country Cottage Inn is the only rental facility that permits pets to stay on the premises—a rule I employed once I was given charge over this place. I've always appreciated animals a bit more than I've appreciated humans, partly because I've never met an animal who has had a bad thought. If my strange gift has given me anything wonderful, it's been the ability to read the minds of animals.

And I never shy away from striking up a conversation with them. The great thing about it is people never question your sanity when you're talking sweetly to a cute furry little creature. And my love of animals is what inspired me to open the inn to pets as well. It's a crying shame more places don't invite responsible pet owners to bring along their fur babies. In fact, I took it one step further and opened up a pet daycare center in the back of the inn.

That's exactly how Country Cottage Critter Corner was born. To be honest, Critter Corner is truly the star of this place. We have an entire facility attached to the back that has both an indoor and outdoor area that allows ample room for the animals to roam within their respective areas. We get as many cats as we do dogs and bunnies alike.

The entire inn feels like my baby through and through. But I'm not the owner, and to be honest, I think that takes the pressure off me. The owner of the inn is actually a wealthy earl who lives in England. We met once and the rest of our correspondences have been over the phone or through emails. And to be honest, I like it that way. It almost feels as if the inn and the surrounding properties are mine. And when I'm not running the front desk, or minding the grounds, checking on boarders, or paying the bills, you can find me in the café wishing that I could bake right alongside the pastry chefs, because as my moniker suggests, I do like to whip up a sweet treat in the kitchen now and again—even if it does end in catastrophe.

The waves slap over the shore almost violently, reminding us that summer is a quickly fading dream and fall is upon us. It's mid-September and tonight is the farewell to summer bonfire, right here at Cottage Shores, and everyone in Cider Cove will be here.

I head down to the waterline in haste. It's my job to make sure the beach is clean, cleared of any unwanted debris, and that there is more than enough chopped wood brought in to feed the hungry fires that will dot the sand later this evening.

Fish jumps in front of me. ***It's so beautiful here. Why must the people come and ruin everything?***

I can't help but giggle at that one. "You have no idea how many 'people' feel exactly that way."

I take a full breath as I look out at the expansive cove itself with its pristine belt of sugary sand that caves in like the letter U. An embankment of maples, sweetgums, ashes, birch trees, and oaks ensconces us on either side as they stand tall and proud, almost right to the waterline on either side of us. Their leaves have already turned colors of burnt orange, deep gold, and fiery red. There is no place as magical as Cider Cove in the fall.

The wind picks up, causing the ocean to churn like a washing machine ready to hit the spin cycle.

Fish trots out about three feet ahead of me and freezes. Her long fluffy fur stands on edge in a ridge over her back as she looks wide-eyed and terrified down to my right, and I turn my head that way just in time to see a white and red freckled dog bounding this way at a million miles per hour, and, just like that, Fish darts to my left in a blur.

"Fish!" I scream as I run out a few feet to my left, but no sooner do I dart in her direction than she's already dashed past me the other way. The rather large dog barks up a storm with his tail pointed up and ears standing erect as he does his best to chase her.

"No! Stop! *Fish*!" I howl in a tizzy as my sweet cat bolts my way, and just as I'm about to catch her, she zooms right between my legs and so does that pesky pooch, knocking me off balance in the effort. "Oh no!" I buck backward and trip over a piece of driftwood. My legs do a little tap-dance as I try to regain my footing, but it's no use.

I land smack on my bottom in the wet mushy sand as water pools around me in what feels like a hostile foamy display.

"Oh no." A sense of panic grips me as I struggle to rise. The memory of being trapped in that whiskey barrel comes rushing back uninvited, and suddenly every muscle in my body threatens to paralyze with fear. I struggle to rise just as a wall of water engulfs me from behind and I'm left gasping and reeling as I get sucked out to sea a good ten feet.

Can't breathe!

Can't see, think, or feel.

It's as if every nightmare I've ever had has suddenly come to life and sprung on me from behind in the form of a killer wave.

"*Hey!*" A pair of arms gesticulate wildly as a man with dark hair wearing a full three-piece suit wades in cautiously, yet quickly, in an effort to give me a hand. "I've got you!" he shouts as I flail and gasp, trying my best to find my footing as another wave crashes overhead—this time right over the two of us.

"*Geez!*" he shouts as he clasps his hand onto mine. Only, instead of pulling me toward shore, a swell pulls us both out farther in the opposite direction.

"Help!" I scream at the top of my lungs, but with the wind picking up and the violent waves sloshing around us, I can hardly hear myself.

My feet lose their grip of the bottom and my body demands to move with the wild current, but I'm holding onto the man in his nice three-piece suit as if he were a life preserver.

"Swim with the horizon!" he shouts as he does his best to reel me in, but the violent swells have an entirely different idea.

"I'm going to die!" I shout as I do my best to hoist myself back in the direction of the shore where I spot both Fish and that naughty freckled cutie pie, who thought it was a good idea to give a chase in the first place, both seated a safe distance from the waterline as they watch us struggle our way to safety. "Fish! Call for help!"

"*Duck!*" the man in the three-piece suit shouts and I get pulled under as another hostile wave crashes overhead.

We cork back up to the surface and he reels me in tight, wrapping an arm around my waist, and I see him for the very first time. My heart detonates just once at the sight of him—dark hair plastered to his head, gorgeous bone structure, a peppering of dark stubble gracing his cheeks, but it's his eyes—I've never seen such light gray eyes. They're stunning. And in turn they add a breathtaking allure to his already comely features.

Beautiful. Just that word alone roams through my mind and a breath hitches in my throat at the thought.

For a moment, it's as if all of time stands still and those glowing eyes of his are conducting a takedown of all my good senses.

"Are you all right?" His voice is husky and firm, and there's a hard look in his eyes and, dare I say, an air of superiority about him in general.

He's good-looking and he knows it. I'm far too familiar with his type. But he has a scholarly appeal to him, and something about him screams the fact he's been wounded a time or two. I try to steady my gaze over his to see if I can get a read on his thoughts, but there seem to be too many components distracting me at the moment.

"Never been better." I'm not sure why I spouted the lie. Considering my wet and wild predicament, I've never been worse.

Another wave slaps over our heads and we're sucked out to sea once more before being propelled at inhuman speeds in the opposite direction as the ocean vomits us back to shore.

"Oh, wow," I pant as I get on all fours in an attempt to gain my bearings. "We survived. We're not dead." I claw at the sand as I inch my way farther from the hostile water.

"Of course we're not dead. Come here," he groans as he struggles to rise himself and he gives me a hand.

"Thank you," I say and I'm about to introduce myself, or hyperventilate from the trauma that just occurred, when

I spot that freckled dog growling at Fish, and Fish bravely standing her ground as she makes sure I've survived my seaside adventure. "Oh no, you don't," I say, charging my way back to dry land. "My cat is not a snack or a toy or anything in between."

The dog bullets down the sandy stretch of the cove and the man in the sopping wet suit takes off after him.

"*Sherlock*!" he shouts as he runs lethargically, and I do the same as I head for the inn.

"Come on, Fish," I say and she lets out a hair-raising roar before hopping like a bunny all the way back to the Cottage Café.

I'll see you there, Bizzy! she calls out. *I may never venture near the shoreline again. And so help me, if I see that beast again... On second thought, so help him.*

Trust me, Fish, I never want to see the shoreline again myself.

I'm sure I could easily convince Fish to relocate—but only after she exacts her revenge. I'm sure of it.

It's going to be a long, soggy day, and I'm already wishing I could head back to my cottage and swaddle in a blanket in front of a roaring fire with a good book and a cup of hot cider.

After I wring myself out, I carefully make my way back into the building. The inn itself is cavernous inside, with wooden floors distressed in a gray and white marbled color. There's a large grand staircase that leads to a second level where most of the rooms are located. The doors and wainscoting, along with the counter that frames the front of the expansive foyer, are a rich dark wood heavily inlaid with carvings. There's a large event room on the south side of the building that's seen just about every celebration you can imagine and a formal dining room for the guests of the facility. The Cottage Café on the east end of the building leads right to the sandy shores of Cider Cove and is open to guests and to the public as well.

Fish is already seated on her favorite perch, the white marble counter that spans the front of the reception area.

Emmie bats her inch-long lashes my way in horror. Emmie and I look as if we could be sisters with the same long, wavy, dark hair, same frosty blue eyes, olive skin, and pouty lips. We happen to share the same formal moniker as well, *Elizabeth*, but we've devolved in different directions with that one. When I was born, Macy, my older sister, couldn't say my name properly, so Bizzy it was. And Emmie was an adorable nickname that her mother gave her and it simply stuck.

"What happened to you?" She trots over with a box of tissues and dabs the water from dripping off my nose.

"I thought I'd make sure the ocean was still salty and wet for the party tonight. Check and check," I say as I make my way to the front desk and run my eyes over the ledger quickly.

"Oh my goodness, Bizzy!" Emmie sucks in a quick lungful of air as she quickly puts the traumatizing pieces together. "Are you all right? Can I get you something? A cup of hot coffee? An apple walnut cinnamon roll?"

I can't help but give a weak smile at that last one. That was my newest brainchild, the very dessert I dreamed up and tried to bake but turned the entire batch into a pan of rock-hard Frisbees. Thankfully, Emmie took my suggestion and it's been a hit at the Cottage Café all month.

But, before I can answer, the bell chimes at the entry, and in through those oversized doors comes a heart-stoppingly handsome man in a soggy suit and a leashed freckled beast striding in by his side, and I can't help but give a wry smile at the two of them.

Emmie leans in so close I can feel her body heat beginning to warm me. "Mother of all things holy. Can I keep him?"

"I'd say yes, but I think he's bad luck," I tease—mostly.

He smirks at the thought. "I'd contest that theory." His pale gray eyes needle into mine. *I'm pretty sure you're the one with bad luck, sweetie.*

I gasp as if he said the words out loud.

See what I mean? Prying into people's minds is a hazard of a superpower no one should be privy to.

"I beg your pardon?" I'm quick to contest it. "My innocent cat was minding her own business when your lumbering beast decided to chase her into the ocean."

The poor pooch whimpers and sulks as if he understood me, and I have no doubt he did.

The man straightens. The muscles in his jaw tense a moment, and it only gives him a meaner, sexier appeal, and I want to scream and throw things because he only grows more obnoxiously handsome by the moment, and perhaps more obnoxious in general, too.

"My beast was simply following his instincts." ***Those blue eyes, though. I could stare at them all day,*** he says internally as he openly inspects my features, and I can feel my cheeks heat up ten degrees at least.

Does he like my blue eyes? Most likely he likes Emmie's blue eyes, but—he is looking right at me. I try to pry into his thoughts to see what criticism or disparaging remarks are lurking around up there but there don't seem to be any.

He flexes a wry smile my way. "Who do I see about checking in?"

Fish saunters over and sits between us as if she were showing up for duty.

Don't do it, Bizzy, Fish warns. ***Tell them to find shelter elsewhere. Like Connecticut.***

I wrinkle my nose at my sweet cat before clearing my throat.

"That would be me," I say, tapping over the keyboard until today's check-in file pops up on the screen. "Name, please."

"Jasper Wilder," he grunts it out as if he were angry at the fact.

Emmie giggles as she hovers over my shoulder.

"Jasper Wilder," she whispers into my ear as if it were a secret.

"Yes, I heard." I bite down over a smile. Emmie and I happen to have a soft spot for the quasi-vampire related name.

I glance down the list of names due for arrival today and note in horror he's leased the cottage in front of mine.

I suck in a quick breath. "You'll be a resident?" I look up at him and he blinks a satisfied smile.

"That's right. I've leased a two-bedroom with a fenced yard."

"Wow, that's—just great." I have a feeling Fish will never let me hear the end of it. "What's your pooch's name again?" I say, hiking up on my tiptoes to get a better look at him from over the counter, and the poor thing is crouched low with his eyes pinned on Fish as if he feared for his life— as he should. Fish might be small, but she is mighty.

"Sherlock. Sherlock Bones." His lips curve into a smile as Emmie giggles herself into a conniption.

"Sherlock Bones!" She pokes me in the ribs. "That's so clever. Isn't that clever, Bizzy?"

"Bizzy?" His dark brows bounce as if my name amused him. I can't say I blame him. My name has amused people for over two and a half decades now.

A warm laugh bounces through me. "That's right, Bizzy Baker. And this is my cat, Fish," I say, nodding her way. "I'm the manager here at the Country Cottage Inn. And if you need anything at all—"

"Ask for me." Emmie snaps the key to his new home off the dowel next to her. "In fact, I'll take you both to your cottage and make sure you're well acclimated."

Jasper looks my way, his icy eyes searing over mine, and try as I might, I can't get a bead on what he's thinking. It's as if he knows what I'm capable of and has suddenly erected a shield over his mind. Not that it's possible, and not that I should be too concerned about his errant thoughts that may or may not be complimenting my eyes.

I bite down over my lip as I look his way once again. Fine. I might be a little more than interested to know about his errant thoughts. He's a looker. You'd have to be dead not to notice how arrestingly handsome he is. And judging by how fast my heart is pounding at the thought of him, I'm certainly not dead.

They're halfway to the door when a thought comes to me.

"There's a bonfire on the beach tonight! All guests are welcome to come."

He turns my way and grunts in lieu of a response, and I grunt right back like a knee-jerk reaction.

I watch as Emmie chats away a mile a minute as she leads him and his adorable dog to their cottage.

"Jasper Wilder," I mutter under my breath.

He's far too ornery and perhaps far too handsome for my taste.

I catch a glimpse of him through the window as he walks farther from the building. He pauses for a moment, turning my way, and my heart thumps wildly as if contesting my protests.

"He's not the one for me," I insist.

Is he?

2

There is no more of a majestic sight than Cider Cove in the fall. Well, it's almost fall, thus the giant banner strewn across the front of the Cottage Café that reads *Farewell to Summer Bonfire!* The café itself is attached to the inn with the rear dining patio that butts up to the white powder sand.

Emmie and I have spent the remainder of the afternoon, and the early evening, tending to every last detail, including pre-packing the s'mores kits that are such a hit on this night every year.

An entire mass of humanity has poured out into our tiny corner of the world just in time to witness a glorious citrine sunset. A live band plays from a platform constructed over the sand just down the way from the inn, and it's wall-to-wall bodies as they sway to the music.

I made sure to keep Fish at home for the night. There will be far too many people for me to ensure her safety, and I want to do just that.

She made it no secret she wasn't pleased to be left out of the festivities, but I gave her a few treats along with her Fancy Beast cat food in an effort to make it up to her. Fish has been such a delight to me in the last few months since she's been in my life. I feel just as protective over her as if she were my child. I can't imagine having an entire human to care for twenty-four seven. Lord knows, a furry child with a mind of her own is about all I can handle.

Emmie rocks her hip into mine. "So when is Jasper getting here?" *You know you can't stop thinking about him.*

I balk at the thought. Emmie might be my best friend since childhood, but she has no idea that I'm capable of reading her mind. As afraid as I might be of water or tight spaces, I'm ten times more terrified of the masses finding out about my not-so-cute little foible. Reading minds isn't a cute hobby or a zany quirk. It's an invasive ability that no one should be capable of. As much as I love Emmie, she can't keep a secret to save her life. And since it's my life on the line, I thought I'd spare her the trouble of trying to keep it under wraps.

"I'm not thinking about him." I suck in a quick breath once I realize I just responded to her mind rather than her question. "I don't know if he's coming. I simply extended the invite his way. We'll see what happens. And before you go there, every guest is invited tonight and you know that."

"Jasper Wilder," she says it low and husky as if trying his name on for size. "Do you think he's a vampire?"

A few years back, both Emmie and I were obsessed with a young adult book series that featured a rather sexy vampire with that very name. I must admit, it's not a moniker you hear very often—unless, of course, you're speaking of the aforementioned fictional vampire.

"Vampire?" an elderly female croaks from behind and my spirit brightens at the sound of that warm familiar voice.

"Now look what you've done, Emmie. You've woke the dead," I tease as I turn to find Georgie heading this way. Georgie has long gray hair intermingled with a dusty brown shade. Her face is relatively smooth, save for a smattering of crow's feet, despite having already spent eighty-two years on the planet, and she's dressed head to toe in a sparkling pink and black kaftan, her signature attire.

Georgie Conner is the one person who knows about my so-called gift—a complete accidental gleaning. And yet, she seems to genuinely appreciate it, too.

"There are no vampires, Georgie. I can assure you of that." I pull her in for a quick embrace and my nose twitches as we part ways. Georgie reeks of something and it's not her usual spiced cinnamon perfume.

"You like?" Her eyes are wide as she nods as if trying to get me to go along with the farce. "Here"—she shoves an armpit in my face, and I inch back, nearly tripping over a potted plant—"don't be shy! It's a new patchouli deodorant from Lather and Light. Macy is letting me test-market the stuff. Get a good whiff. You, too!" She aims her weaponized kaftan Emmie's way.

"No, thank you," Emmie says, fanning the air between us. "I'm sorry, but it smells less like anything the Lather and Light would sell and more like your latest kill."

Not only is Georgie a celebrated artist who specializes in mosaics, but she's an avid hunter as well. In the grand scheme of her nutty granola-ness, it almost seems contradictory in nature, but she insists she's a proponent of thinning the herds.

I've known her for going on a decade, and she's yet to kill a single thing. That's what I like best about her.

"You don't say *kill*." She wags her finger at Emmie. "You call it *dinner* and you thank the creature for feeding you before you put it in your mouth. Now back to the topic at hand. When did we get vampires? I've been itching to hang with a coven."

"There are no vampires," I whisper.

Georgie waggles her brows. ***There are and you know it. Save a couple cute ones for me, would you? I have a thing for being bitten after midnight.***

A giggle brews in my chest because I have a feeling it's true.

I lean in. "No vampires for you, Georgie. And we should probably keep it down. It's bad enough the entire world believes this place is haunted."

"Well, it is." Georgie doesn't mind perpetuating the lie. "Everyone knows that Leo De Camps, the dude who built this place, killed his family and cemented them into the walls. There's a big write-up on Wikipedia. I should know. I put it there myself." She grins at Emmie and I gasp.

"Georgie! You did not!" But honestly, I wouldn't put it past her.

"You gotta keep this place going, sister. If it goes under, both you and me are out of a place to live."

"And me," Emmie chimes in.

Georgie waves her off. "The vampires would have drained your blood by then."

"Funny." Emmie takes a moment to scowl at her. "And I'm not the one dating the vampire. It's Bizzy."

"No!" Georgie's bright red lips round out as if she just heard the juiciest bit of gossip.

"Yes," a male voice says with just as much enthusiasm as Jordy, Emmie's older brother, steps up. "And what am I protesting?"

Jordy is handsome in a boyish way, has a round face and big, sweet blue eyes—but he's a ladies' man who has no intention of slowing down. I may have accidentally married him in Vegas three years ago, but our drunken matrimonial union lasted all of twenty-four hours—without the benefit of a wedding night, might I add.

As soon as we got home, my brother Hux, a prominent divorce lawyer in Seaview County, took care of the unfortunate circumstances. Who knew Hux would come in handy when I needed a divorce myself? Technically, it was annulled, and both Jordy and I were none the worse for wear, but Emmie nearly didn't forgive either one of us for the matrimonial blunder.

Jordy tips his head our way. "What's got you twisted in a knot?"

Georgie steps in. "Vampires. And Bizzy is dating one."

The sound of glass breaking deep in the café disrupts the conversation, and Georgie's artistic antennae go up.

"I think I'm about to collect some valuable supplies." She lifts a finger and heads in that direction. "If you'll excuse me." *And by the way—I'm looking into someone who might know something about your special ability to voyeur into other people's minds.*

31

I think you're going to love him. He lives in a yurt behind a dairy farm and he's going to look into your predicament. But don't you worry. He won't breathe a word.

I cringe at the thought. Yurt aside, the fact he's looking into my predicament is terrifying.

"Don't worry." Emmie sighs as she takes off for the kitchen. "I'll make sure it gets cleaned up."

Jordy's brows sharpen with concern.

Jordy is one person whose thoughts I'm not interested in prying into. I came to this conclusion after discovering he has a propensity to envision the two of us in a variety of compromising positions.

He squints over at me. "Are you really dating a vampire?"

"He's not a vampire. He's a man named Jasper, and we're not dating. Believe me when I say the man is not interested in me in the least."

"Well then, he's clearly not in his right mind." Jordy folds his enormous arms over his chest. Jordy is in charge of groundskeeping here at the Country Cottage Inn. He used to work in upper management out in Seaview County but suffered a nasty breakup with one of his female bosses and landed here at the inn with Emmie and me and never got around to leaving.

"You're funny," I say as I scan the crowd for any signs of my family, and, instead, I spot the tall, dark, and handsome questionable vampire. "Oh, look!" I swat Jordy on the arm. "The fanged night dweller is headed this way."

"The one you're not seeing?" He's suddenly amused as he narrows his gaze on Jasper. "He looks like trouble. I'd stay away if I were you. And I take it that's his dog?"

"Ooh! He brought Sherlock Bones?" I hike up on my tiptoes and crane my neck as I struggle to see this for myself.

"Sherlock *Bones*?" Jordy's voice drips with disapproval, but before he can vocalize it, the sound of arguing erupts from our right and I spot one of my waitresses, Kaitlynn Zimmerman, just past the café patio in the sand, arguing with someone.

"I'd better get over there before this turns ugly." I scoot off in their direction as their disagreement grows more heated.

Kaitlynn is a cute strawberry blonde with a head full of wild kinky curls, and the biggest brown eyes you ever did see. She's been with us for about six weeks, and I've never had a single problem with her. And my goodness, tonight is the one night I would never fire a soul—not even if she's in the middle of telling off a customer.

Please Lord, don't let it be a customer on the receiving end of this wild rant of hers.

"Kaitlynn?" I call out as I traipse my way into the sand. "I'm sorry. Is there a problem I can help you ladies with?"

The girl next to Kaitlynn stands almost a head shorter than her with long dark hair and watery turquoise eyes that shine under the duress of the twinkle lights from the café.

I try my hardest to get a read on her thoughts, but she's either far too agitated or she's an outright restriction. Every now and again I'll meet someone whose thoughts are safely tucked away in their own Fort Knox.

"I'm sorry, Bizzy." Kaitlynn readjusts her apron before looking my way once again. Her eyes settle on mine. *Please don't fire me. I need this now more than ever. Just a little bit longer, and I'll make it over the hump.* "I was just having a rather uncivilized conversation with my stepsister. Bizzy, this is Rissa McNeil. Rissa, this is my boss, Bizzy."

"Bizzy." The brunette suddenly has a smooth countenance as she extends her hand, and I shake it. "It's a pleasure to meet you. I'm sorry to take any of Kaitlynn's time. I'll be enjoying the bonfire if you need me." Her eyes harden over her stepsister's once again before she takes off, and if I didn't know better, I'd say that was a threat.

"Wow"—I say as we watch her get swallowed into the crowd—"that looked pretty heated. Are you okay?"

Kaitlynn shrugs it off. "It's par for the course between the two of us these days. She's just angry because my friends are here tonight, and they don't always get along. And let's just say someone I know happens to be dating her boyfriend Ben." She nods. "You heard me right."

"Ouch. That's gotta hurt. So, I take it she'll be avoiding your social circle?"

"Not likely. We share the same friends." She nods to the bonfire to our left, last one on the sand, next to the ridge. "I'll catch up with them after my shift. That is, if Rissa hasn't slaughtered anyone by then." She laughs as she heads back toward the café. "Enjoy your night!" she calls out as she gets right back to bussing tables.

"Excuse me," a deep voice rumbles from behind, and I turn to find the most delicious, and, might I add, dangerous, gray eyes pressing into mine.

"Mr. Wilder." I straighten at the sight of him. He's casually dressed in jeans and a flannel. His hair is slicked back, and the woodsy scent of his cologne warms me from the inside out. Sherlock trots forward, and I moan as I offer him a scratch behind the ears. "My, aren't you the cutest? Yes, you are! Did you try to chase my sweet kitty right into the ocean today? You are one silly boy. You look guilty. Yes, you do!"

I apologize. The adorable pooch with the big brown eyes looks my way. *Next time, I advise she stand still so I can wrap my mouth around her properly.*

I gasp at the thought.

"I'm afraid I'm guilty, too," Jasper says, and I'm quick to stand upright again.

"Excuse me?" I'm quickly lost in those bewitching gray eyes. It's as if he has a lightning bolt trapped in each one. Mesmerizing.

"I want to apologize for being curt with you this afternoon." His lips pull back with a tight smile, but it doesn't last long. "I'm not usually so insufferable, but—"

"But you were soaking wet—and in a three-piece suit no less. Please, no apology necessary."

He shakes his head, a tiny comma-like dimple erupting amidst the scruff on his cheek. "I'm apologizing regardless. Let me make it up to you." He opens his mouth to let me know exactly how he'd like to do so when someone shouts my name from behind.

"Oh no," I whisper under my breath as Hux and my mother come upon us.

Huxley, *Hux*, is essentially a male version of me, same dark hair and pale blue eyes. He's not only a divorce lawyer, he's currently on his third marital dissolution. No kids from any of his wives, and at this point I'm grateful for his sake.

My mother is a sharp cookie who used to run her own real estate empire but has since sold her business last year and is still trying to find her place in the world. She's not exactly cut out for retirement.

Hux examines Jasper a moment. "Is this the vampire you're dating?"

Kill me.

Mom leans in. "Open up and let's see your fangs."

A choking sound emits from me as I spin my mother in the other direction. "Macy is by the s'mores station, and she says she's in need of desperate advice on how to run her business."

"I knew it." My mother lifts a bony finger in the air. "I told her she needs my sage advice, but she didn't believe me." She migrates into the crowd and I look up at Jasper with an apologetic shrug.

"That was my mother, Reeann Baker, just Ree for short. And I apologize for the latent introduction."

Hux clears his throat. "So this is the vampire."

"He is—but he isn't." I grimace up at Jasper. "And to answer your next question, we're not dating."

Jasper offers a crooked grin my way. "I'm the vampire?" He cinches the leash in his hand and Sherlock Bones sits up at attention as if he were wanting the answer to this as well. "It's okay. I've been called worse." *And why*

aren't we dating? His expression sours as if I've insulted him.

"Hux Baker." My brother is quick to shake his hand. "Family law. If you're in a mess with the missus, I'm your man." He gives a cheesy wink before migrating toward the crowd on the sand. "Nice to meet you. Don't let my sister scare you off! Her bark is worse than her bite."

"He's kidding," I say. "My bite leaves marks, and it's only doled out upon request." My cheeks burn as the words leave my lips. "I'm sorry. That was extremely inappropriate of me. Have you seen the s'mores buffet?" I'm quick to point him in that direction before I slink off into the shadows to lick my wounds.

I'm about to make my way around the building, through the sand, when I trip over something far softer than driftwood. I quickly regain my footing and bend over to remove whatever it is out of the pathway lest someone breaks an ankle and sues the inn, but it's not a piece of driftwood or anything remotely I could move on my own.

Every muscle in my body freezes as my eyes lock on the familiar face lying beneath me.

It's a woman—and one I know all too well.

Kaitlynn Zimmerman isn't finishing her shift after all tonight.

Kaitlynn Zimmerman is dead.

3

A shrill scream rips from my throat as I try my best to keep from falling in the sand.

The sound of the wind and the blaring music from the other end of the beach drown out my horrific cries, but that doesn't stop me from repeating the effort.

"*Bizzy*?" a deep voice thunders from my left as Jasper hurtles a planter box to get to me. His hands gently clasp over my arms, dropping his leash in the process as Sherlock runs a circle around us. "What's wrong? What's the matter?" His piercing eyes seem to glow in the dark, but not a single coherent word comes from me.

I look to the sand and he follows my gaze.

"Oh no." He kneels down and checks for a pulse before jumping to his feet and whipping out his phone. "This is Detective Wilder. I need to report a homicide. The victim is a young woman, mid-twenties, multiple stab wounds to the chest. I need assistance at the Country Cottage Inn, and get the coroner down here now." He shoves his phone into his pocket as he makes his way back to me. "Are you okay?" His eyes run up and down my body as if looking for wounds on me as well.

"I'm fine. I just—I tripped over her body." My hand clamps over my mouth as I look over at my sweet friend. "That's Kaitlynn Zimmerman. She works for me at the café—*worked*." That last word comes out in a whimper. "Did you say you were a detective?"

"Homicide division. I work for the Seaview Sheriff's Department. Don't worry, Bizzy. I'll take care of everything." His gaze presses into mine. ***I will do whatever it takes to protect you,*** he says it internally as if he were speaking the words straight from his mouth.

An entire herd of deputies head in this direction and Sherlock jumps between us barking up a storm.

Jasper picks up the leash as the deputies swarm around poor Kaitlynn.

"I hate to ask you this"—he winces—"but would you mind watching Sherlock for me? I need to be a part of this."

"Absolutely." I take the leash from him and Sherlock whimpers as if he were just sold for a handful of beans. "Are the guests safe? Should we close down the beach? What about the inn?"

"That's entirely up to the sheriff, but I'm guessing in the least you'll have an infantry of deputies flooding the area. You'll be safe, and we'll do our best to keep your guests safe, too."

He steps away, and sure enough the café is promptly closed and the entire inn is overrun with deputies combing through it.

Emmie runs over, her face piqued with color. "What in the world? What's this about a body?"

"It was Kaitlynn." My voice breaks as I say her name. "Someone stabbed her to death and took off." My voice trembles. "I found her."

Emmie pulls me into a hard embrace, and we lose it for a moment before trying our best to sniff back our emotions.

She glances at the deluge of deputies who only seem to be multiplying. "I'm going to cover the front desk. Why don't you take a walk by the water and try to pull yourself together as best as you can?"

"No, I need to be here." I try to break my way past her, but she blocks my path.

"Hit the beach. Take a short walk and then you can have the reins again. It's going to be a long night, Biz. And you're going to need a clear head." Her lips press white a moment. "I'm sorry you found her." She offers me another quick embrace before pushing me in the direction of the shoreline.

Sherlock pulls me toward the water as if he were bent on following Emmie's directions himself.

"Just so you know, Sherlock"—I lean over and give him a hearty scratch over the ears—"I can hear your thoughts and understand you." I meant to whisper it but with all the noise and confusion around us, I can guarantee no one heard a thing.

His head turns briefly my way. *You can hear my thoughts?*

"Yes, I can." A sorrowful laugh strums from me. Typically I'm ecstatic to have an exchange like this but I'm so rattled by what just happened to poor Kaitlynn, I can't derive joy from the moment.

Sherlock belts out a few quick enthusiastic barks as he barrels down the beach.

"Whoa," I say. "Slow down, boy. I'm not on a sled, you know."

I'm sorry, but the water seems to call my name over and over. And if I'm anything, I'm obedient. That was a horrible sight and I need to get it out of my mind. Poor Jasper had to stay behind. Do you think he'll be safe?

"He'll be safe," I say as we navigate our way through a thicket of bodies. "I'm assuming he's armed and dangerous himself. I can't believe he's a homicide detective," I say that last part lower than a whisper.

We thread our way through the crowd, and the smell of driftwood burning fills the air with its musky scent. Usually, I look forward to this night every single year. The bright flames dotting the shore, the trill of laughter, the cacophony of voices exploding all around. The delicious smell of hot dogs roasting mingling with the sweet hint of marshmallows burning is a strange elixir that lends a certain level of magic to this already magical night.

Kaitlynn runs through my mind and I shudder. I doubt I'll ever see our end-of-summer bonfire in the same light again.

"Bizzy!" a familiar voice calls from the left, and I spot Georgie waving me over. Mom stands next to her, speaking with Macy, and my feet take me that way of their own volition.

I glance back toward the Cottage Café where the deputies have descended upon the inn. To the right of the building, the flashing lights of patrol cars sear through the darkness, but with the live band going and the growing number of bodies swelling all around, you would never know we were all a part of a homicide scene.

Georgie tips her chin down, and she's got a look on her face that suggests I've been up to no good. "There's our

Bizzy, *Bizzy* girl. How was your date with the sexy vampire?"

Sherlock yelps as if contesting the fanged idea.

Macy's brows hike into her forehead upon hearing the seemingly juicy tidbit of gossip.

"Did she just say *vampire*?" She takes a step in my direction as does my mother.

Macy has a short razor cut bob that curves along her jawline, and she dyes her dark brown locks a vanilla shade of blonde. She shares the same watery blue eyes as I do, same button nose, but Macy is a bit more no-nonsense about life in general than just about anyone I know. Okay, fine, she's mean and cranky and sarcasm is her superpower—and, oddly enough, I love all three of her ornery attributes.

"Don't mind me." I'm quick to wave my mother and sister off. "Please continue with your conversation." I give Sherlock a quick pat on the head as he struggles to press into the crowd without me.

Mom huffs, "Macy was just enlightening me on something called FIRE, financial independence, retiring early. Apparently, the new hip thing to do is quit your job and live in a yurt while calling it an early retirement. Please tell me this is an anomaly and not something that's sweeping through your generation. My generation depends on your generation to keep its act together. The world economy is shockingly in your hands."

Georgie waves her off. "She's just bitter she didn't think of it first. Hey"—she leans in my way, and I get a whiff of that experimental patchouli she's donned in the name of hygienic science and my sister's bottom line—"did you hear your mother is seeing her podiatrist?"

I can't help but wrinkle my nose at the thought. "Sounds like a stinky situation."

"Ha!" Macy barks. "That's what I said." The smile glides right off her face. "Now who's this hot vampire, and how much do I have to pay him to take a bite out of me?"

Georgie slaps her on the arm. "You can't have him. Bizzy found him first." She looks back my way. "I bet he sleeps upside down and naked in the closet."

Mom scoffs. "Where did you dig this one up? A janitorial closet at the inn?"

"You're not far off." I shrug. She had the part about the inn right.

Sherlock barks at something down the way and tugs at the leash as if he's ready to charge in that direction. I glance over and spot a loud boisterous group congregating around one of the bigger bonfires, and I recognize the girl with the kinky curls as she knocks back the contents of that oversized red cup in her hand. That's Rissa, and those must be Kaitlynn's friends. That's the bonfire she pointed out to me earlier in the night.

"Excuse me for a minute," I say as I let Sherlock lead the way, and Georgie shouts after me, something about wanting a proper introduction to my four-footed friend when I get back.

"Where are you taking me, boy?" I whisper as if I didn't know, and sure enough, he slows down as soon as we near the loud crowd.

"Hey, it's you!" The girl with the curly hair waves me over. "It's me, Rissa." Her words slur slightly. She's barefoot and staggering as she struggles to gain a solid stance in the sand. It's dark out here, save for the glow of the towering fire and the moonlight dancing over the ocean as far as the eye can see. "I want to apologize for my little outburst. Kate and I get along most of the time."

My heart breaks when she mentions her stepsister, and I don't have the heart to say a word about her recent demise.

A tall gentleman steps up. He's handsome in a conventional way, light brown hair, heavy tan.

"Is this about Kaitlynn?" He tips his head my way, suddenly concerned, and it makes me wonder if he's already been told.

Rissa smacks him playfully on the stomach. "Never you mind." She looks my way. "This is Chris Davidson, Kaitlynn's fiancé—worrywart extraordinaire."

A breath hitches in my throat at the revelation. This poor man is going to be devastated.

I clear my throat. "Nice to meet you. I'm Bizzy Baker. I run the inn." Sherlock barks as if he wanted an introduction of his own. "And this is my friend, Sherlock Bones. I guess you can say I'm dog-sitting for the night." Because his sweet fiancée is dead, and the owner of this dog just so happens to be the lead homicide detective. But I would never breathe a word. And suddenly I feel terrible for keeping such a grim secret from these people. I'd better have the sheriff's department come down and break the news to them.

A brunette about my age jumps over and kneels in the sand at Sherlock's feet, and soon he's licking her face, and if I'm not mistaken, he seems to be licking away her tears.

"Is everything all right?" I couldn't help but ask. It could be that the killer is right here in this social circle. Maybe even this girl who's sobbing in front of me. Why else would she be hugging Sherlock as if her life depended on it? It's clear she's distressed over something.

Rissa takes a deep breath as if she were exasperated. "That's Sammy Walton. She had a dog just like this. They practically grew up together. She still gets emotional when she talks about him. I'm guessing you'll have a hard time separating those two for the rest of the night."

"That's so sad. I completely understand." And here I had all but accused her of murder.

"Seeing that you're Kaitlynn's boss, I feel the need to be extra nice to you." She gives a devious smile my way. "The consensus around here is that you should give her a raise." Her entire body shakes as she belts out a warm laugh. And under normal circumstances I would join in, but these are far from normal circumstances.

The whoop of a siren breaks through the music, and everyone around the bonfire cranes their neck in the direction of the inn.

Chris, Kaitlynn's fiancé, staggers from side to side, trying to get a better look at it.

"Something's happening." He glances to his left and nods at someone in the crowd, and my adrenaline kicks in for a second time tonight at the strange behavior.

"*Eh.*" Rissa shrugs as she takes another sip from her plastic red cup. "Probably just someone who got in someone else's way. Happens to me all the time." She knocks back the rest of her drink before dissolving into the crowd.

A dazzling blonde steps over and brazenly picks up Chris' hand. Judging by the way her body conforms to his, it doesn't appear she cares too much about the fact he's seemingly engaged—*was* engaged. Not that he knows it's past tense at the moment.

"Bizzy Baker," I say as I extend my hand her way, and she laughs as she glides her own hand up Chris' shirt instead.

"Come on." Chris plucks it out and slightly redeems himself in my eyes. "My apologies." He nods my way. "She's toasted."

They take off for a chaise lounge where she falls onto his lap.

"He doesn't seem to mind the attention," I say to the girl looking longingly into Sherlock's root beer-colored eyes.

A dull laugh bounces from her, and I can smell a plume of vodka emitting from her breath.

"He never does," she says. "That was the problem with Kaitlynn. She never did understand how this crowd works." She hops to her feet and takes off down the beach, and I'm left holding my breath at what she just said—or rather the manner in which she said it.

I turn and stare at the girl until she's swallowed by the crowd.

"Oh my goodness," I whisper. That girl just referred to Kaitlynn in the past tense.

Sherlock pulls me along, and I let him until we hit the boulders at the edge of the cove. I kneel down and offer him a hearty scratch between the ears.

"You're a good boy. I'm so sorry you had to see that tonight."

His eyes lock onto mine, and there's an ease that goes along with it. It's that specific feeling that lets me know I'll have no problem prying into his sweet mind.

It was a terrible sight. The things humans are capable of never cease to astound me.

"Hey?" I whisper. "What do think of the fact that I can hear you?"

Sherlock gives a quick bark that quickly morphs into a howl.

"That's right. I can hear your thoughts as easily as if you were speaking them," I whisper as if a cast of thousands were hovering over my shoulder, but we're far enough from the crowd for me to be too concerned about who might see me having a full-blown conversation with a cute little pooch. Besides, half the population speaks to their pets. I've never had a single person call me out on my strange behavior. "That girl back there that couldn't get enough of you. I think they said her name was Sammy. Could you tell if her tears were genuine? I mean—as far as mourning a pet goes?"

They seemed to be. He whimpers. I could feel her grieving deeply. ***Those tears were wrenched from the depths of her soul.***

"Yes, but who were they for? Her old four-footed pal or Kaitlynn? I mean, was it really a coincidence that she mentioned Kaitlynn in the past tense?"

"Excuse me?" a male voice says gently from behind and I jump up in fear, only to discover it's an all too familiar homicide detective.

"Detective!" My hand clasps over my chest. "You nearly scared the pants right off of me."

His cheek flickers. ***Now there's something I'd much rather be doing.***

My mouth falls open. I don't know whether to be affronted or giddy.

"It looks like the two of you were having a great conversation." His shoulders broaden, and it only seems to increase his masculine appeal. His lips twitch as if they want to smile, but the night and all of its sins aren't permitting it.

"Sherlock has some very good things to say. You should really try to listen sometime. Did you catch the killer?"

He winces as a dull laugh bounces through him. "Not yet. But we will. We just need some time."

"While you were up there, guess where I was? Right in the thick of Kaitlynn's social circle."

"What?" His brows narrow into a hard V, and it's not difficult to tell he disapproves.

"Yeah, I spoke to her stepsister and she introduced me to Kaitlynn's fiancé. A total philanderer if you ask me. He acted as if he expected something to have happened to her, and then when he heard the sirens, he nodded to someone in the crowd. Isn't that weird?"

"Wait." His hands bounce toward his temples for a moment. "Did you seek these people out? Did you happen to mention anything that just happened?"

"No! No, Please no. I figure you have to adhere to protocol, notifying next of kin and all. But, in all honesty, Rissa might just be the next of kin. Anyway, there was this girl named Sammy, and she said some really strange things—and she talked about Kaitlynn in *past tense*! I bet she's your killer. She went that way." I nod down to the opposite end of the cove. "I can help you find her if you want."

"I don't want." His eyes harden over mine, and suddenly his mind closes off like a steel trap. "This isn't some play investigation. This is all too real. And for your sake, I don't want or need you getting involved. There is a very dangerous killer out there, and I'm betting they'll stop at nothing to cover their tracks." His chest palpitates as if he were suddenly out of breath. "Look, I came down here to let you know that we need to cordon off a part of the inn. Let's get back to the scene and you'll do your job and I'll do mine. I apologize if this sounds harsh, but I'm giving you a directive to stay out of my investigation."

Sherlock whimpers as if apologizing for the ornery human before us.

"Your investigation." I nod up at Jasper with a frown. "Got it," I say as we head back toward the inn together.

Detective Jasper Wilder.

I think I liked him better as a vampire.

4

September in Cider Cove is usually fraught with leaf peepers descending upon us from every corner of the country.

The splendor of nature erupts in a riot of color as the leaves give way to the art of dying. The maple leaves from the embankment above the cove have already shaken loose and are tumbling down the beach in front of the café in a parade of citrine color. The ocean is a dark hue of navy as the wind has its way with it, turning the entire sea into a bevy of whitecaps. But that doesn't stop anyone from walking along the shore, bundled as they might be in cozy sweaters and scarves, a cup of hot coffee or the requisite *cider* in their hands. Yes, fall is majestic in Cider Cove, and it's always been and always will be my favorite season.

Last night was a nightmare within a nightmare. In fact, when I pried my groggy eyes open this morning, I had hoped it was exactly that, just a very bad dream. But once Sherlock Bones hopped onto my bed and licked my face as he tried his hardest to tug me to the door, I realized last night's horror was a very real thing.

As soon as I got home, Sherlock chased poor Fish around for a solid fifteen minutes before Fish pounced on him from the side and walloped him with a paw to the face. Sherlock tucked his tail between his legs and promptly went to sleep on the rug in front of the fireplace, and for the most part they got along just fine after that.

Jasper never did come by last night. Although, I didn't expect it. He doesn't know where I live. I'm sure he had a long night himself, so I don't mind keeping Sherlock. I would have happily taken him to Critter Corner this morning, but seeing that I don't have Jasper's permission I couldn't do it. Instead, I let him out onto my courtyard before I left and made sure he had plenty of water. I even gave him some of Fish's cat treats so he wouldn't go hungry and he seemed to appreciate it. Heck, he told me as much. I wish all human minds were as easy to read as animals', but it's rarely ever that way.

The inn is nearly booked to capacity, and I've staffed the front desk so that I can officiate one of my favorite duties on the grounds, working in the café. I've given Fish stern orders to stay near the outdoor patio. There's a mound of flowers, balloons, and teddy bears growing to the right, in the exact place where I found poor Kaitlynn's body last night. This might explain the sudden spike in customers streaming in and out of the café all morning.

Emmie finishes up at the counter and exhales hard as she heads my way. "I need to brew some more coffee. We've sold more pumpkin spice lattes today than we did in all last year."

"Tell me about it," I say as I restock the glass shelves with a fresh supply of Danishes and croissants. There is a pumpkin roll to die for, complete with a cream cheese filling that I dream about all year once it's taken off the menu. And now that it's back, I'll have to purchase an entire roll just for myself. In fact, I'd like nothing more than to lose myself in all things pumpkin rather than thinking about the awful way Kaitlynn died.

Emmie has her dark hair pulled back into a ponytail, her olive skin looks practically luminescent, and she doesn't wear a stitch of cosmetics to enhance her beauty because she doesn't have to. She's just that beautiful. And even though Emmie is essentially a goddess among humans, I've never felt intimidated by her beauty. Emmie is as gorgeous inside as she is out. It's just another facet that demonstrates my best friend is impeccable at everything—even the genetics she can't control.

"Who do you think did it, Bizzy?"

I frown out at that area of the sand and note a crowd gathered in the area. A couple of young girls take a moment to pet Fish. I have a tag on her collar that not only states her name and my number, but the fact she's an employee of the Country Cottage Inn. And so far, that's been enough to keep her out of the wrong hands. However, she's wily enough for me to believe she can wiggle her way out of just about anything.

"I don't know who." I quickly spill the strange events that occurred last night—the argument, Kaitlynn's fiancé, and her friend's odd behavior at the bonfire.

Emmie shakes her head. "It sounds like the Seaview Sheriff's Department has more than enough suspects to bring this investigation to a quick conclusion. And, thankfully, that hot vampire of yours morphed into an even hotter detective last night. He questioned every single employee—and don't you think for a minute that every woman on staff wasn't plotting on how to snag more of his attention."

"He questioned me briefly, too." And before I can process the fact every woman here is suddenly interested in garnering his attention, Georgie and Jordy walk through the door.

Georgie is wearing an oversized kaftan that all but dusts the floor in her wake. It's cranberry in color and has gold and bronze thread woven throughout. Not only is Georgie an artist, but she prefers her clothes to be sort of an installation piece as well—and that's exactly why she makes them herself. Her long gray hair is frizzy and flowing just the way she likes it, and she's donned her signature bright red lipstick.

"Bizzy! How was the date with the sexy vampire?" Her eyebrows waggle suggestively.

Emmie scoffs as she pours them both a cup of coffee. "It ended in murder."

"Murder!" Georgie clasps her hands together. "You know what they say—

that's good luck."

Jordy frowns, looking every bit like his sister in male skin. "Nobody says that, Georgie." He settles his eyes over mine, his expression suddenly far too sober. "What happened, Bizzy? Emmie told me that you found the body."

I spill it all again, minus the detail about having a rather nice conversation with Sherlock. The only person who knows about my ability is Georgie, and I only told her in a fit of frustration after she accused me of reading her mind—and, of course, she was right. Georgie's mind is pretty open, so reading it has not only been a breeze, but she's helped me hone my skills by trying to shield her thoughts in different ways while I try to unlock it like a puzzle.

"Geez." Jordy takes a quick sip of his coffee. He's got his jeans and flannel on, his usual uniform for taking care of the grounds. And since he's a looker, he's amassed a bit of a fan club around here. Jordy hasn't been serious about a girl in so long, I think he's forgotten what the parameters of a relationship should look like. It's safe to say he's Cider Cove's resident playboy. "If one of her so-called friends was responsible for her death, I can't imagine what kind of a callous heart would then go down to the bonfire as if it never happened."

Georgie lifts a crooked finger. "One that wanted to cover his or her tracks."

"You're right," I'm quick to agree with her. "But they all seemed like excellent suspects. And to think, I only met a handful of them. I wonder what the rest are like."

"Hey!" Georgie's baby blues widen like hardboiled eggs. "Maybe it's some cult that needed a virgin sacrifice for the upcoming autumnal equinox? I bet it was the fiancé. It's always the fiancé. Once that sun crosses the celestial equator, who knows what he'll be able to get that homicidal harem of his to do next."

Mom walks in just in time to hear that last tidbit and groans hard. She looks sharp today with her hair puffed and feathered, highlighted and coifed to perfection. She's donned a fitted pantsuit in the perfect shade of eggplant and has a matching cardigan tied around her shoulders.

"Georgie, Porgie, your mind is pudding and pie and filled with nonsense." She shoots her a curt look. My mother and Georgie have a love-hate relationship at best. "It's time for our staff meeting at Lather and Light. Are you ready to try to talk my daughter off retirement's ledge?"

"Why would I do that?" Georgie cinches a tote bag over her shoulder.

"Because she's not even thirty."

Georgie is quick to wave her off. "Not even thirty is the right time to retire. Take it from me, I should know. That's exactly when I started to get off the grid." She gives a wink my way. "Don't you tell any of those juicy vampire tales until I get back." *I want the dirty bits, too. And if there aren't any dirty bits, I suggest you take a clue from your name and get busy.*

"Very funny," I mouth over to her as I try my best to stifle a laugh.

Jordy points to a pumpkin muffin, and his sister is quick to ring it up for him.

He nods my way. "Since when are your mother and Georgie on Macy's payroll?"

"They're not," I say. "Macy wanted a board so she developed one. Sometimes I think her true destiny of working in Manhattan was derailed by way of wax detail." It's true. When the old owners of Lather and Light put the store on the market for just about free, Macy snapped it up as nothing more than a potentially lucrative business endeavor. Her heart has never been into soap or candles. "Emmie, could you send a group text to all the employees at the inn? A psychologist is coming down from Seaview County, and she'll be around this afternoon if anyone feels they need some extra help to cope with the tragedy."

"Will do." She gets right to prattling away on her phone as an all too familiar face pops into the café and I cringe.

"Mayor Woods." I offer a short-lived smile, mostly because as the manager of the inn I'm obligated to be kind to visitors and mean girls alike—even if they did land me a supernatural gift.

"Bizzy." She offers a tight smile right back.

Mackenzie Woods is a tall brunette, light eyes, big toothy two-faced grin, and an ego the size of the solar system. Mack's the aforementioned reason I have this supernatural gift or curse as it were. Suffice it to say, I've never played bobbing for apples with her or anyone else since that fated day she nearly drowned me for kicks. I wasn't too crazy about her need to steal my boyfriends either. So after Emmie and I parted ways with Mack back in high school, it seemed we jumped off the social ladder altogether and Mack kept right on climbing until she was the queen bee—mean queen bee. I'm not sure what sponsored her hatred of me in general, but whatever it was

I'm betting it happened right before that nearly fatal bobbing for apples fiasco.

Just last year her father stepped down as mayor of Cider Cove, so she ran during the last election and won by a landslide. I think the good people of this town appreciated the nostalgia she offered with her name alone. And let's be honest, promising to increase parking on Main Street was a draw, too. Everyone knows parking anywhere in Cider Cove can be murder. Which is exactly why I ride my bike or hoof it whenever I can.

"Mayor Woods. What can I do for you?" I don't mind giving her the professional due she deserves. I've called her worse.

She saunters over, shoulders back. She's donned a tweed blazer with ruffled edges and a fitted pair of slacks. Mack looks like she could be a model in one of my mother's preppy-wear-for-older-women catalogs.

"Bizzy. *Jordy.*" She offers him a flirtatious smile. Honestly, I think Mack is the only woman I know that Jordy hasn't sunk his teeth into. And if he has, I don't want to know about it. She looks my way. "I thought we could start a new tradition here in Cider Cove and have the orchards and artisans and everyone in between come down to the cove to share their wares. We'll call it the Harvest at the Cove Festival. And on behalf of the event, I wanted to ask if the Cottage Café would be interested in hosting a booth."

"I love it!" Emmie gasps as she trots on over. "We can set it right outside the café itself and naturally draw in visitors. We'll have dessert and a few savory treats as well. Miniature versions, of course. That way if they want more, they'll have to come on in."

I nod to Mack. "It sounds great. We'll be glad to do it. In fact—" Before I can say another word, an arrestingly handsome homicide detective walks on in and takes my breath away. He's wearing a dark inky suit and has those comely gray laser beams he sees the world through pointed right at me.

Mackenzie follows my gaze. "Well hello, stranger. Mayor Woods at your service." She extends a hand, and he politely shakes it. "What can I do for you? Please keep in mind that I do aim to please." *I'll land this one horizontal by midnight*. Her devilish grin expands. *Official plus one or not—he doesn't stand a chance.*

Plus one or not? It would figure she doesn't care if he has some poor wife tucked away somewhere. Mack is despicable.

My blood boils in an instant, but I try my best to let it go. This is simply Mack being Mack. For Pete's sake, she can't know that I'm interested in him.

Wait. I'm not interested in him, am I?

He bows slightly. "Nice to meet you. Detective Jasper Wilder. I'm in charge of investigating the homicide that took place here last night. In fact"—those glowing gray eyes pierce into mine—"I was hoping to speak with Bizzy."

Mack's eyes widen in horror as she looks my way. She quickly wiggles her way in front of him and fans her hair back.

Hair-tossing stunt aside, Mack is stunning, and to be truthful, I'm not so sure I like her looking so stunning around Jasper.

"My office is open to you at any time, detective." She shoots a wry look my way. "As soon as you're done here, please feel free to stop by. I'm on the other end of Main Street. I'm sure Bizzy and her husband will offer all the assistance they can to help further the case along." She winks my way. "I'll speak to you girls later." She scuttles off, and if I didn't know better, I think I just saw her fly off on a broomstick.

Jordy expands his chest as he looks to Jasper. "Watch yourself." He offers a hardened stare that reads as something just this side of a threat before taking off.

Emmie gives me a slight shove from behind. "Go on. I'll keep an eye on the inn—and Fish, too."

I take off my apron and make my way around the counter.

"I believe I have something of yours at my place," I say as I fight the urge to smile like a loon. I so hate the fact I'm interested. A man like Jasper is far too handsome for both his sake and mine. The odds are in his favor. He knows this and I bet he's a master at exploiting it.

Her place. His lips curve at the tips with wicked intent, and I'm quick to blink my gaze in another direction lest I end up in places of his mind I'm not ready to delve.

"Perfect," he says. "And then maybe after that, we can grab a quick bite if you don't mind? I'd like to ask you a few more questions."

A date *and* an interrogation?

It sounds par for the course, considering how this week is shaping up.

On the bright side, I'm still breathing, which is more than I can say for poor Kaitlynn.

She wasn't just my employee. She was my friend. And because of that, I'll do whatever it takes to track down her killer.

Including sacrificing my afternoon to spend a little time with the most gorgeous man to grace Cider Cove since its inception.

Sometimes you have to take one for the team.

5

Just up the road from the Country Cottage Inn is a plethora of shops and restaurants that line all of Main Street.

Jasper and I picked up Sherlock and decided to take him along for the walk.

"That's my sister's shop," I say, pointing to the big picture window outside of Lather and Light. There's a silk wisteria tree inside, and it adds a magical appeal to the establishment.

"Lather and Light." Jasper steps back as he reads the gilded signage. "I like it. Smells nice, too."

Every shop in Cider Cove has a wrought iron frame filled with gilded letters. It's all a part of keeping up with the cobbled streets and stone front buildings that look as if they've been here for hundreds of years. And most of them have.

I point up the street. "Our dining options are about to creep up on us. There's a cozy diner coming up that serves amazing burgers. It's a fifties themed restaurant complete with shakes and shoestring fries. There's a great pizza place to the left. Chinese and Thai to the right. And then there's the Sand Witch—you can't go wrong with their sandwiches and they have an outdoor eating area with space heaters. We could sit with Sherlock and keep warm."

"That sounds good to me. How about you?" His gray eyes press into mine. *I'm getting hungry, all right.* His lips curve at the tip, and I can feel my face heat twenty degrees. That's the hazard of prying into someone's mind— you're liable to hear just about anything. I can control it on my end, too. But it's rare for me to turn down the volume. And I've never judged anyone for their thoughts. It's certainly not my business what goes on in their minds— even if I make it so. And I get it. Just because you think it doesn't mean you'd verbalize it out loud. Not for the most part anyhow.

"A sandwich sounds perfect. But don't blame me if you get addicted. The Sand Witch is one of Cider Cove's biggest draws. So, what brings you to our little corner of Maine anyway?"

"My family is from Sheffield, just between Ellsworth and Bar Harbor."

My mouth falls open as I laugh. "You're local enough then. But what brings you to Cider Cove?"

"Work." He nods as we come upon the shop and we tie up Sherlock outside before heading on in, and once inside the delicious scent of marinara sauce and fresh cut vegetables hits our senses.

"*Mmm*. That settles it," I say. "I'm going for the eggplant."

He glances at the menu. "I've got to have the barbeque beef."

We put in our orders, and soon we're right back outside with Sherlock as we find a small round table next to the outdoor open fireplace. The liquid ambers that line Main Street send their leaves tumbling around us in a display of cardinal and gold, and the crisp air reminds us that fall has ushered summer right out the seasonal door.

"Go on," I say. "You came for work. Did you transfer?"

"I did." He winces and manages to look painfully handsome in the process. I'm not sure I've met a man like Jasper before, so sure of himself, seemingly kind and normal, and yet every woman at the surrounding tables has already stolen more than a glance in his direction. "I transferred to Seaview from Sheffield. But full disclosure, I had a bad breakup and wanted a fresh start."

"Oh, I'm so sorry." I glance to Sherlock, and his eyes zero in on mine.

Don't be. Sherlock sniffs and nods toward my food. ***She was a shrew who never shared her food with me.***

I take in a quick breath before pinching off a piece of my bread and casually dropping it to the ground.

"So what happened?" I lean in, returning my attention fully to Jasper. "Can I ask?"

"Absolutely," he says as we both start in on our meals. "Mmm, this is insane. You're right. The addiction has begun." He blinks a quick smile, and my stomach bisects with heat. Jasper is so comely, half the women here keep turning around to steal a glance at him. "It was a mutual parting. I think we just outgrew each other. We were together for about four years. She moved on, and I moved out. She's a counselor at the local high school, and she"—he flicks his fingers as if struggling for words—"started dating one of the deputies. I wanted to give them space—and I think I needed it, too."

"That must have been hard—the dating your co-worker part. I can see why you'd want to make an exit."

"How about you? The mayor mentioned you had a husband."

I can't help but avert my gaze to the sky. "*Had* as in past tense, and you've met him. Jordy and I were married for less than twenty-four hours. It was a poor choice sponsored by Jim Beam and a drive-thru wedding chapel in

Vegas. Believe me when I say I haven't had a sip of anything that toxic since."

He chuckles at the thought. "I would definitely suggest you abstain if you're prone to run to Vegas and tie the knot."

"My brother Hux, the one you met last night, is in family practice. He helped me get it annulled rather quickly. But yes, our dear mayor has a propensity to bring up my flaws. And if you lend her an ear, I'm sure she'd love to fill you in on whatever dirt on me she happens to have." She's made it a habit to dig for dirt on yours truly, and Lord knows she's never had to dig that far. She's had a front-row seat in my life for as long as I can remember. Nevertheless, Cider Cove doesn't keep secrets very well. And that's precisely why I haven't told anyone outside of Georgie about my special abilities. Who knows what would happen to me if word got out? I'd probably be living in some governmental cage for the rest of my life.

A shiver runs through me at the thought.

"Ouch." His dark brows frame his glowing eyes. "I take it you and the mayor have a history."

"A tainted one. Silly high school stuff that should have ended there. But now she's the mayor, and I'm her not-so-devoted constituent." I shift uncomfortably at the thought of Mack weaseling her way into our conversation. I should know better than to give her a spotlight, so I quickly change the subject. "Any news on who could have killed Kaitlynn?"

His eyes linger over mine, but I can't key in on what he might be thinking.

"Considering the violent nature of the crime, I think it's easy to deduce this was a crime of passion."

I suck in a quick breath. "As in that fiancé I met last night was guilty?"

"I can't say. I've seen this play out in many ways. I know you gave me a quick rundown on the three people you met last night, and I've already questioned Chris Davidson and Rissa McNeil. I haven't spoken to Sammy. Was there anything else you might have seen last night? Anything out of the ordinary now that you've had a moment to think about it?"

"Everything was out of the ordinary last night. I mean, we don't have the entire town and every tourist in Maine pouring out onto our shorelines each night. There was a cast of thousands, and it was my job to make sure that the inn was in top condition and the café was well-stocked for the onslaught. All of the waitresses were on edge, but they knew what to expect. Most of them anyway. Kaitlynn had only been working for us for a couple of weeks, but she caught on quickly and everyone liked her. She was easygoing and funny, too." I try to think back on anything that might have sent up a red flag but come up empty.

"Do you mind if I ask what her last place of employment was?"

"Not at all. I didn't process her application. Emmie did, but I can pull it up for you if you like."

"I'd appreciate that." He grimaces. "And just so you know, it's been confirmed that the knife—the murder weapon belonged to the Cottage Café."

I gasp. "She was bussing tables. My goodness, she could have had it in her hand. How terrible that someone used it against her like that."

"It is certainly terrible."

My curiosity is about to get the better of me once again. "What did her family say? Did her fiancé or her stepsister provide any information about her?"

He's about to take a bite out of his sandwich and pauses. "I'm sorry, Bizzy. I can't share any of that information with you."

I choke on my next words. "But if we work together, we might be able to find the killer twice as fast. She was my employee. I might be able to help you crack the case."

A dull laugh bounces from him. "No way. This is an active homicide investigation, and a dangerous one at that. The killer could be anywhere. They could be a guest at the inn for all I know. There's no way I'd place a civilian in any more danger than necessary."

A chill rides up my spine at the thought. "A killer right under my nose? Under my *roof*?"

Sherlock whines as he lies on the ground and lands his paws up over his ears as if he didn't want to hear it himself.

"Whoa, I'm sorry, Bizzy." Jasper dips down to catch my gaze. "You and your guests will be safe. I'm beefing up the area with deputies until we're sure we've apprehended whoever did this. And I will bring them to justice. I can promise you that."

"That's a big promise."

I'd promise this girl just about anything.

A small laugh rattles in my chest. "Thank you."

"It was nice meeting your family. And your grandma Georgie, too. She seems like a real character."

"That she is. She thinks you're a vampire."

"Strangely enough, I get that a lot."

We share a warm laugh at his blood-sucking status.

"Georgie isn't actually my grandmother. I acquired her in the divorce—my father's divorce. He's on his fifth, and I think she belonged to wife two or three. Anyway, Georgie's daughter married a wealthy count, and the two of them have been sailing the Mediterranean on his yacht ever since. And I kind of fell in love with her, so when the apartment she was living in was condemned, I offered her a studio cottage just behind the inn and she gladly snapped it up. She sells her mosaics to cover the rent. They're beautiful. I'd love to show you her work sometime."

"I'm in. My sister is an artist—mostly acrylic, but she dabbles in oil paint. She lives in Rose Glen."

"Nice. Does she have a studio? Is she showing her work? I'd love to drive Georgie over some time to see it."

"She has a showing coming up in October. You're both more than welcome to come. You'll be my guest."

"Then it's a date!" And just like that, I wish I could bite my tongue off. "I mean, on the calendar—not like you and me. But a threesome. You and me and Georgie. And, oh wow, that sounds even worse. I'm going to shove this entire sandwich into my mouth now." And I proceed to do just that, but Jasper is too busy chuckling to do the same.

"You know, you remind me a lot of my sister."

I stop mid-bite.

Mark that under *words you never want the cute homicide detective to utter*.

Did I just say that? His entire expression grows momentarily distressed.

"What I meant was, sweet and innocent."

"I can assure you I'm not that sweet. Ask any of my employees." I shake my head. "And just to clarify, I don't actually own the inn. It's owned by a wealthy earl from England. His name is Quinn Bennet, and he has more important things to do than run the inn, so he's hired me to keep an eye on it. I pretty much came in right out of college. I managed the café, and once the old property manager left, I was grafted into the position."

He offers an affable smile. "So, where'd you go to school?"

"Dexter." My cheeks burn with heat. This is probably the part where I should fess up and tell him I didn't graduate, but I can't seem to bring myself to do it. "I studied business, and you?"

"You're a Dexter girl. I like that." His brows furrow as if he doesn't. "I went to Ward."

A laugh sputters from me. "Well, this friendship was nice while it lasted. While I was at Dexter, I had to take an oath not to speak to boys from Ward." Not entirely untrue. Ward was and still is Dexter's most reviled rival. I didn't think I could actually hate an entire educational institution until that century-long rivalry seeped into my soul the very first day I matriculated into the student population.

Jasper laughs at the thought. "At Ward we like to take the high road. We are certainly allowed to speak to girls from Dexter. We're just not allowed to bring them home to our mothers."

"*Ooh*! You went low, detective."

He winces. "That I did. Forgive me?"

"It depends if you're buying coffee."

And he does. Jasper and I grab a cup on the way back as Sherlock trots happily between us.

We arrive at the inn and Fish is the first to greet us, swatting her paws at Sherlock as if she were about to teach him a lesson.

"I'd better get back to Seaview." He nods toward the parking lot. "Thanks for grabbing a bite with me. It was nice." *Very nice. Too nice, in fact.*

I can't help but smile. "Then we'll do it again."

"You're okay breaking faith with your oath? The no talking to boys from Ward?"

"What can I say? I'm a rebel. Besides, I would never hold it against you for not having good taste in educational institutions."

A laugh growls from him. "And she keeps the zingers coming."

"I'll get that application to you as well. In fact, I'll track down her stepsister and see if I can glean anything new."

"No." Any hint of a smile dissipates from him. "I meant what I said, Bizzy. Stay away from this investigation. This is not for you." *Don't even think about it.*

I scoff at the thought. "Well, I'm certainly thinking about it."

He blinks back as if I struck him, and my fingers fly to my lips. I've made it a practice not to repeat a thing I've heard anyone thinking—except for this instance. But I couldn't help it.

"Please don't think about it." He sighs as if he were resigned to the terrible truth. "I'll see you later."

"Enjoy the rest of your day, detective."

Jasper hops into his truck with Sherlock at his side and they take off.

I don't need anyone telling me what I can and cannot do.

Least of all a boy from Ward.

I'm going to talk to Rissa McNeil. And I bet I'll get a heck of a lot further with her than he ever could.

Boys from Ward, indeed.

6

The nerve.

The next day, try as I might, I can't seem to get that ornery detective out of my mind. And, worse yet, in succumbing to his greedy ego's desire to take over my gray matter, my ability to pry into other people's minds is on overload.

Here she comes again. Let's see what fault she can find with me this time. Asher, Jordy's groundskeeping assistant, glowers at me a moment before offering a seemingly kind hello.

For the record, I have not found fault with him once. I've found fault with the fact he's left the gardening clippings out all afternoon last week for the guests to see and heaven forbid trip over. I actually enjoy Asher's company. He's one of the only people who shares my affinity for hot cider with a dash of cayenne pepper.

"Hey, Asher!" I offer him a friendly wave. "I've got a hot cup of spicy cider with your name on it waiting for you in the café!"

His features smooth out as he offers a genuine smile. "Sounds good, Bizzy! I'll head in as soon as I dump today's clippings!" *That Bizzy—you can't help but like her.*

A smile bounces over my lips. Now that's much better. The last thing I want is for my employees to see me as a tyrant. I love the inn, but more than that, I love the people who make up the inn.

Fish and I head to the check-in area, where she promptly finds her bed behind the counter and curls up in it.

I make sure the front desk is well-staffed. Both Grady and Nessa, a couple of recent college graduates, are working the early shift with me today.

They've both made it explicitly clear that I understand they're simply slumming at the inn until their real careers kick in.

Grady is a clean-cut, dark-haired playboy with milky white teeth and hypnotic blue eyes that makes all the guests under thirty swoon with his inherited Irish charm. Emmie affectionately refers to him as the eye candy up front.

And Nessa is a gorgeous brunette with skin that nature kissed the color of a perfect latte. She's smart as a whip but far too obsessed with everything but the inn. Nessa's older sister, Vera, went to school with me at Cider Cove High. She was pretty much a mean girl who lived to make my life miserable, and it looks as if her sour attitude toward me has trickled down to her not-so sweet little sister. Nessa and Vera also happen to be first cousins with Emmie, hence the nepotism that helped land Nessa the job in the first place.

And in keeping with today's chaotic theme, they both barrage me with their thoughts at once.

I hope I get tickets to the big game tonight. Man, I live for Sea Raven football, Grady says as he pretends to be intensely studying the daily guest stats on the monitor before him, but I'm guessing he's on StubHub or Rip Off Seats 'R Us. *And if I do get the tickets, I'll have to call in tomorrow*. He glances my way. *I feel the stomach flu coming on. She won't want me here for days.* His eyes grow wide at the screen. *He shoots, he scores.*

I take it he got the tickets.

Nessa smirks over at his screen. *Perfect. Once he's gone, I can finally relax. I'm so tired of him judging me for reading. Who cares if I'm reading on the job? It's not like there's anything to do while I wait for the slow trickle of check-ins and check-outs. Besides, my book challenge is to read a book a week. I've got other people in my book club who are keeping tabs on me. I need to make this look effortless.* She glances my way. *What is she staring at, anyway? Creepy. It's like she's reading our minds or something.*

"You're both doing a great job," I say. "Nessa, have you read *Where the Apples Fall*? It's the number one pick in the library's book club this month." Her eyes widen a notch. "And Grady? My father always has an extra set of tickets for the Sea Ravens. I can get you a set if you like."

He looks a little green around the gills as he gets back to tapping on the keyboard. I'm guessing he's gunning for a refund—and I hope he gets it. I don't mind one bit that Grady wants to head to the game. I'd love to make his dream come true. He's a nice guy and a hard worker. I'd love for him to stay on staff well into the future.

"Let me know if you're interested," I say. "But we'll need you here tomorrow, if you don't mind. We've got a leaf peeping tour pushing through."

He perks right up as the screen before him displays the words *refund initiated* across the top. "I don't mind at all, Bizzy." He sighs with relief. "And please thank your dad. I can't wait to get to the stadium."

"You bet! I'll arrange for the tickets to be sent to you in a few hours."

I take off for the café and pick up on the melee from the customers at the tables.

Darn weather is too cold for me. I knew booking a getaway at the shore this time of year was a lousy idea. Way to waste my money and my vacation days.

The French toast is to die for. I'd give my eye teeth if my wife could make this at home. Hey? Maybe if I ask real nice they'd give me their secret recipe? Doubtful. I'd probably have to throw in a dying mother to sweeten the pot.

I hear there's mini golf just behind the orchard. The kids would love that. And I'd do anything to tucker them out for once.

Honestly, days like these, when I'm being inundated with the thoughts of the world around me all at once, are rare. It really does take something—or someone as, well, irritating as Detective Jasper Wilder to agitate me just right to initiate this nightmare. And, unfortunately for me, this can take some time to subside. So, I do the only thing I can. I pour myself a pumpkin spice latte and head deep into the kitchen to find my best friend.

Emmie glances up from the island where she's pouring batter into pans, and from the orange patina of it and the hint of allspice, I'm guessing she's making her famous pumpkin rolls. They truly do hold the scent of sugar and spice and all things nice. They're the personification of fall if ever there was one.

"I get first dibs," I say as the kitchen staff runs to and fro around us, their thoughts in a flurry.

Am I burning this?

Did I remember to make that?

We're running low on potatoes. We need to beef up the order.

I make a mental note of that last one.

Emmie flashes her baby blue peepers my way. "I'll give you the whole roll if you give me all the juicy details of your lunch date with the hot resident vampire."

"He's all bark and no bite." I can't help but scowl at the thought of him. "Can you believe he insisted I stay out of his investigation?" I lean in and whisper, "I mean, Kaitlynn was our friend. She's just some *body* to him. He wants her application, and I said I'd give it to him."

"That's because you're a pushover." She gives a sly grin. "Come on, Biz. He's a cop. He doesn't want you turning up as the next victim. I get it."

"I get it, too." Kaitlynn and her beautiful smile come to mind, and it breaks my heart all over again. "But, I'm the one that saw her having a heated argument with her stepsister that night. In fact, I found the body, and I spoke to her friends first. Technically, he's the one who's infringing on *my* investigation."

"You're not investigating."

"I'm not. I'm simply going to track down her stepsister, Rissa, and ask her a few questions."

She stops mid-flight with a pan in her hands, and I head over and open the oven door for her—that's about the only thing I can do right in the kitchen.

"What kind of questions?" She drops the pan in with a bang and shuts it.

"Just a few basics like who, what, where, when, and why."

She makes a face. "And then after you regale her with your basic journalistic skills, do you plan on tazing her and dragging her to the nearest sheriff's department?"

"No. I plan on dragging her all the way to Seaview and tossing her on Detective Wilder's desk like the catch of the day."

Emmie groans, "You never could resist a dare."

"He did not dare me to find the killer."

"Not in so many words."

"I don't care about words, or about Jasper Wilder. I care about justice. Now, help me track down Rissa or I'll be forced to employ Georgie in on the effort."

"Good Lord." Emmie tips her head back. "Do not drag Georgie into this, or all of Cider Cove is liable to end up slaughtered in their sleep." She sighs deeply. "Fine. But I'm strictly going to avoid the aforementioned massacre. Do not even think about nosying around with any other suspects. I'm sure Rissa won't mind too much. We'll turn over Kaitlynn's belongings that she left here that night."

"Belongings? What kind of belongings?"

"A jacket and her purse. Jasper asked about her things that night, but I didn't know where they were. It turns out, she placed them under the chair in the office. And since he hasn't asked about them again, it's only fair we give them to her family." She makes a face. "Or the killer."

"Or the killer. Right." I glance to the office, suddenly itching to get some clerical work done.

Emmie leans in. "How are we going to find Rissa?"

"I'll try my best to stalk her on the internet. It's Rissa McNeil." I straighten as the kitchen staff propels itself around us. "You know, I think I need to beef up the order. I hear we're low on potatoes." I smile over at the kitchen staff and they look mildly relieved. I step in close to Em. "And I think I'll review Kaitlynn's application while I'm at it."

I head to the office and shut the door behind me, dragging a filing cabinet over a notch to block the entry. Sure enough, a small navy purse and a jean jacket lie neatly folded under the seat at the desk and I pull them both out. My fingers quickly run through her pockets, nothing but a tissue and a stick of gum still in its wrapper. Her purse is loaded with receipts, mostly to the coffee shop up the way, Espresso Yourself, a few for the Thaime for Thai, Cider Cove's best Thai restaurant, the Dragon Express, my favorite place for Chinese, and the Breakfast Bender, a diner that specializes in pancakes bigger than their plates and happens to serve nothing but a breakfast menu all day long. It's a tourist favorite, and it's nearly impossible to get a seat there without being subjected to an hour-long wait. I'm friends with Clara, the woman who owns it, and she always sends her overflow down to the Cottage Café.

"One thing is for sure. Kaitlynn had a hearty appetite."

I stumble upon a longer receipt, one for the local library with about ten books that were recently checked out. I should probably give Dawson down at the Cider Cove Library a heads-up that the books may not be coming back anytime soon. Dawson Brawn is a longtime friend of mine. We dated briefly in twelfth grade before Mack decided she could take him farther in his endeavor to lose his virginity. I make a face at the receipt as I study it a moment.

All of these books are how to start up your own business and succeed at it.

Huh.

It looks like Kaitlynn was dedicated to starting her own business. I wonder what that could have been?

The door to the office slams over the filing cabinet with a bang and I jump.

"Just a minute!" I call out as if somehow this tiny space had just morphed into a restroom. I quickly rifle through the rest of her purse, unzipping the side pocket and running my fingers along it, and something hard hooks to my finger. I pull it up. It's a ring, a platinum looking band with an impressive cushion cut diamond set in the middle. This must be her engagement ring. She most likely took it off to work her shift. For sure, I don't want this to fall into the wrong hands. I should turn this all over to Jasper so Kaitlynn's mother can sort this out. I'd hate for Rissa to get it and hock it for magic beans.

I snap an empty plastic bag off the floor and pile her things in it before sliding over the filing cabinet, only to find Emmie on the other side of the door.

Her brows hike into her forehead. "I'm not amused. I know exactly what you were doing. Did you find anything?"

"Enough diamonds to send us to Hawaii for three weeks. But don't worry. My ego has decided to sit this one out. I'm handing this over to Detective Wilder instead."

"That's too bad." Her lips curl on the side, a mischievous look if ever there was one. She wags her phone between us. "I know exactly where we can find Rissa."

I suck in a quick breath and try to swipe her phone out of her hand, but she pulls it just out of my grasp.

"Where is she, Emmie?"

"You'll never believe it. Clear your schedule for this evening. We're going to have some fun."

I narrow my gaze on her. "What kind of fun?"

"The kind your daddy wouldn't approve of." She gives a tiny wink and I try my hardest to pry into her mind, but both it and she are laughing as she takes off.

Great.

It looks as if I'll be talking to Rissa tonight.

The bag of Kaitlynn's things burns like a hot coal in my hand, and I decide to quickly drop it off at my cottage. No rush in getting this to that obnoxious detective just yet.

And who knows?

I just might have a killer to deliver along with it.

7

Apple walnut cinnamon rolls are a good and wholesome treat to gift to anyone for just about any occasion, but when I tried hauling them along in an effort to give them to Rissa, Emmie gave a concerning, throaty laugh before announcing, "Trust me, Biz. They don't need your buns where we're headed."

Emmie drives us down to Edison, a town that sits directly west of Cider Cove. I can't remember the last time I came to Edison for anything as I take in the sights. We drive by the dilapidated buildings and the tired looking shops that line the avenues and a part of me feels a bit sorry for the place. For whatever reason, Edison has always been a touch unkempt and grungy but still maintaining its big city appeal to those who flock to the area. If Edison has anything going for it, the plethora of restaurants and seedy clubs alone have kept the cogs of its big city life wheels turning.

Emmie parks before leading us across the bustling street.

"Where are we going?" I glance up at the row of retail establishments and restaurants until I spot an adorable quilt shop seemingly out of place. "Please let it be the quilt shop. I'm dying to stock up on new bedcovers. And I bet they have cute fall patterns and Christmas prints. You know I can't resist a good Christmas quilt."

"Maybe for dessert," she says, spinning me around until we're facing the opposite end of the street, and my jaw loosens as I spot a thorny horny establishment called Sweet Cheeks.

A deep groan expels from me. "We're going in there, aren't we?"

Emmie slings her arm around my shoulder. "You bet, sweet cheeks."

We stride on over to the glossy white building where there's an outdoor patio brimming with people. The windows are tinted so you can't quite see in, and as we head inside, the scent of grilled burgers and fries light up our senses. Next to the smell of cookies baking, there is nothing more delicious than the scent of something fresh off the grill.

A bevy of shirtless, quite muscular men wearing red aprons and jeans run around looking hot to trot with any and every one of the female customers, and I can hear Emmie purring like a kitten at the sight of them. The shirtless bonanza is the standard dress code for the establishment, which boasts of its all beefcake waitstaff that are ready and willing to serve up hungry women. Sweet Cheeks is for women what Hooters is for men. It promises a fine dining experience with enough eye candy to satisfy any estrogen-based sweet tooth. The song "It's Raining Men" is on blast, and I have a feeling they play it on a loop.

A blond hottie with a tray of entrees passes us with a greedy grin.

If I'm lucky, the hot chick in the corner will be giving me the exact tip I'm craving. Her number.

Does anyone eat the pork fest? I don't even know why it's on the menu.

One of the waiters, built like a brick wall, glances at my bestie. ***Check out those knockers.***

I make it a point to scowl at him as he glides on by.

"How exactly is this place connected to Rissa McNeil?" I ask, secretly hoping there's been a serious error on Emmie's part. I wouldn't put it past her to take a testosterone-inspired detour on our way to catch a killer.

"She's the brains to their brawn. She's the operating manager of this particular location."

"It's nice to see we've got upper management in common," I quip.

"And hot men," Emmie is quick to add. "Don't forget about that sparkly new vampire fate just threw in your way."

"He's in my way, all right." My entire body tenses just thinking about Jasper, and not in any good way.

A tall, blond slice of beefcake with a nametag that screams MARK in all caps comes up, grinning from ear to ear as if we were the topless ones around here.

"Table for two?"

Emmie's tongue is already wagging. "Let's make it three in the event you feel the need to join us."

He barks out a hearty laugh. "Three it is." He leads us through the brightly lit establishment with its framed photos of muscle men from eras gone by. A large sign hangs against the back wall that reads *Mouthwatering Beefcake at Your Service*.

Lovely.

We're seated and gifted two glossy menus in the shape of the male physique.

Emmie leans in. "I bet this Rissa chick feels like a queen bossing all these hot men around."

"I bet she feels like a shrew. You and I both know men don't like being told what to do."

"Not the men I date. I think they rather appreciate it when a woman barks out orders."

"That's because the men you date have a hankering to be mistreated." It's true. "In fact, it wouldn't surprise me one bit if a blast from your past—"

Emmie hops out of her seat. "Oh my sweet, sassy stars. Grayson! Is that you?"

A beefy wall of muscles stomps over, bearing little more than a big toothy grin. He's got a capful of black hair and bright, expressive eyes.

"Well, if it isn't Emmie Rose Crosby." He pulls her into a quick embrace. "Where've you been hiding those sweet kisses from me?" *How I miss the things that mouth was capable of.*

I openly frown his way. I'm just one dirty thought away from accidentally on purpose flinging my shoe at him.

Emmie pumps out a guttural laugh. "Oh hon, I'm not hiding. I'm front and center at the Country Cottage Inn right where you left me." She looks my way. "Grayson's family was the one that held the big picnic last June—the one that ended with a beer brawl?"

"Ah, yes." The arrests were a first for the Cottage Inn and the entire clan has since been banned from the premises, but I don't dare say a word. "How very nice to see you again." I think.

He gives Emmie a crooked grin. "Not as good as it is to see this girl. What can I get for you? My treat—the both of you."

I'm quick to protest, but Emmie is equally as quick to thank him and we order up two specials of the day.

"We need some help, Grayson." She leans his way, and I manically shake my head at her. "We're knee-deep in a murder investigation and we need to speak with your boss, Rissa."

I gasp so loud, a ten-table radius turns my way—hopeful that my waiter had just lost his Levi's, I'm sure.

Emmie's eyes grow wild as she clamps her hand over her mouth.

I shake my head up at the wall of muscles.

"We're not investigating anything," I say. "We're here to pass along our condolences to Rissa. Her stepsister was brutally murdered last weekend."

He winces. "I know. She's been very open about it, and we all feel terrible. In fact, we're pooling our tips for the week in an effort to help pay for the funeral."

My mouth falls open. "That's very kind of you."

Here I was relegating them to a bunch of horny devils when they've been nothing but angels with really good abs and pecs all along.

"I'll get your order in and then see if I can find Rissa for you." He takes off and Emmie falls back in her seat, her own cheeks hot with shame.

"Sorry, Bizzy. I guess those big brown eyes of his hypnotized the truth right out of me."

"Emmie, you weren't looking at his eyes. For one thing, they were blue. And secondly, they were due north from where your own eyes were feasting—otherwise known as ground zero."

"Fine. You caught me. But ground zero has a certain appeal."

A shadow darkens our table and we look up to find Rissa with her hair swept up into a knot, her turquoise eyes just as stunning as the night of the murder.

"Can I help you?" She blinks at the two of us as if she were trying to place us.

I offer a pained smile her way. "We met last Saturday night. I'm Bizzy, the manager at the Country Cottage Inn."

"Oh goodness, yes." She falls into the seat between us. "I've been meaning to send a basket of our stud muffins over to the staff. Our honeyed cornbread is to die for." She makes a face. "That certainly didn't come out right." A breath hitches in her throat as she looks to me. "Have they caught the killer?"

"Oh no." I shake my head. "We don't know anything about the investigation. We were just in the area, and Emmie here was visiting one of her exes."

"Grayson." Emmie nods furtively as if this were gospel. "He and I spent a few heated weeks together last summer."

Her mouth falls open. "You're not the cutie from the cove who stomped on his heart, are you?"

Emmie belts out a throaty laugh. "I may have stomped on something, but it wasn't his heart. We were just foolin' around."

"I don't know. I think Grayson had a different perspective." She looks my way. "Just like whoever killed Kaitlynn had a warped version of whatever they think she did to deserve that. In no way did my sweet stepsister deserve what happened to her."

I lean in as if she's about to spill the juiciest bit of gossip. "Did she have any disagreements with anyone that you know of?"

Her eyes slit to nothing. "Yeah. *Me*. But in hindsight, it was pretty silly. Kate and a friend were in the process of starting a skin care and cosmetics line—all-natural ingredients, locally sourced and organic. She borrowed the money for the start-up from my mother, and we had a disagreement over it. I just found out about it last Saturday."

Money? There's a motive for murder for sure, and you don't need to be a detective to figure that one out.

"And, of course, now it's all on Jeannie, Jeanette Branch—that's her business partner—to pay my mother back with interest. It's just a mess."

Emmie leans in, genuinely interested. "What's the name of the company? I'd love to try out some of her products."

Rissa wrinkles her nose. "Natural Beauty is the name of the line."

"And where can we find Jeannie?" I couldn't resist the urge to ask. It's as if some innate part of me is hungry to claw my way to the truth. "I mean, where can we find the shop?"

Rissa sags in her seat. "That's the thing. There is no shop. It was an internet start-up. Right now, all of their inventory is stored in boxes in Jeannie's garage. She lives just past the orchard in Cider Cove."

"The orchard behind the inn? I'm familiar with that tract of houses," I say. "My brother lives there. It's really nice."

"It is. Jeannie has a magnificent trust fund, which is why I was so shocked that Kaitlynn had to borrow any money at all from my mother. But I guess Jeannie was insistent that they each come in with the same amount of money."

"I guess it makes sense. How is your family handling this?"

"Her father is a wreck. Kaitlynn's mother has been a no-show for the last decade of her life. Her friends are understandably grieved." *Not that I'm bawling over this one. Some people get exactly what's coming to them.*

She manufactures a smile my way, and every last part of me freezes.

Grayson comes back with our lunch specials, and Rissa rises to her feet.

"Comp their meals," she tells him.

"I'm one step ahead of you." He tweaks his brows at Emmie before he takes off.

Rissa leans in. "You ladies come by anytime you like. And if you hear anything about the case at all, please let me know." She digs a card out of her apron and slides it my way. "I'd appreciate it."

She takes off, and I'm about to tuck the card away when I spot a familiar dark-haired man looking my way with a pair of ingloriously light gray peepers.

"I'll be back," I say as I whisk over to the bar where patrons are free to sit and enjoy their meal. "Well, look who's here to take in the view." I smear it with as much sarcasm as possible at Jasper Wilder, homicide detective extraordinaire. "See anything you like?" I glance to a muscle man with a signature red apron as he struts on by.

"Funny," Jasper flatlines. *I am enjoying the view. This one*. He bears those steely eyes into mine as if it were compulsory. "I'm more interested in what you're doing here." His chin dips a notch, and suddenly it feels as if I'm about to be admonished.

"I happened to have a hankering for a fresh batch of stud muffins." I flash a quick smile his way. "I'm guessing you got the same urge?"

His lids hang low with the implication, and if I'm not mistaken, he's glowering at me. "I was hoping to speak to Rissa McNeil in an informal setting, but I can see you beat me to it. Care to elaborate on what the two of you might have been talking about?"

I do a quick sweep of the vicinity to make sure Rissa is not around, and happen to note the fact that all the women in here seem to be ogling the one man wearing a suit—the obnoxious detective by my side with the body of a linebacker.

Jasper is a head-turner, I'll give him that.

"No," I say it in the same flat demeanor he just dished it out with, and his head ticks back a notch.

"What do you mean, no?"

"I mean no in the traditional sense. It's an option just like yes, and I choose no."

He's right back to glowering at me.

Difficult and feisty, he muses. ***She's as frustrating as she is cute. Usually not my type. But those eyes. Maybe it's time to start redefining what my type might be. I bet I can get her to go to dinner with me and spill it all.***

"Dream on," I say, but I don't wait for a response, or even bother reveling in the clear look of shock on his face. Instead, I make my way back to Emmie.

Grayson swings by to see how we like the food, and I thank him before politely asking for a couple of to-go boxes.

Emmie leans in once he leaves. "It went that well, huh?"

Before I can answer, there's a hot detective, with an ego that can rival any stud muffin in this place, taking a seat at our table.

"Bizzy"—he starts—"you said Kaitlynn was your friend. You do realize that any evidence you withhold from me is an obstacle to bringing her killer to justice."

Emmie tips her head his way. "Is this about Jeanette... *Jeannie* Branch?"

"Jeannie Branch?" Jasper's lightning gray eyes hook to mine. "You know about her?"

"Natural Beauty Cosmetics." Emmie is quick to nod into her admission.

"Would you stop?" I offer her a sharp kick from under the table, and Jasper jerks as if I kicked him instead.

"Geez." He scoots back, letting me know I missed my target and hit a far more appropriate one. Good. That means my instincts are sharp. "So you got her to open up about Jeannie and Natural Beauty. Anything else you'd like to fill me in on?" He directs the question to Emmie because he knows she's his only hope.

"Not yet." Emmie shrugs my way.

"Not *ever*," I say, picking up our boxes and nodding for Em to follow me to the door. And sure enough, Jasper Wilder is right alongside me.

We hit the fresh air as the beginning of a storm lingers up above.

"I'll see you back at the inn." Jasper glowers at the two of us. "Stay away from Jeannie Branch, Bizzy. You've already tampered with one suspect. Leave the next one to me. The last thing I need is the case unraveling. Please," he implores as his eyes stagnate over mine a moment too long. ***But those lips.***

He shakes his head as he stalks off in the opposite direction.

Emmie tosses a hand in the air. "I guess that's that."

"*That* meant nothing to me. Besides, what's it to Detective Wilder if the spa at the Country Cottage Inn suddenly has a hankering to carry a clean and natural line of products that are locally sourced and organic? I think Kaitlynn would have liked that."

"I think Jeannie will like it even more." She wraps an arm around my shoulder as we watch Jasper hop into his truck.

"I think we both know who won't like it," I whisper.

My lips curve with satisfaction at the thought of disobeying his wishes.

Jasper is right. Kaitlynn was my friend, and I want to see her killer brought to justice.

That's exactly why I'm about to dive into the deep end of *my* investigation.

Next up—Jeannie Branch.

8

The scent of the Atlantic in the morning sears my nostrils with its salty brine, but I take it in by the lungful just watching as the frothy water laps the shore.

It's early yet, the breakfast rush is still in full force, and I'm helping out in the café indefinitely until I can find a replacement for Kaitlynn. I still can't get over the fact the poor girl was murdered—and right here at the inn.

Who could possibly want her dead?

I can understand why people evict one another out of their lives but not by way of removing them from the planet. It's unfathomable.

Fish meows from the benches where the café meets the sand, and I head over as she hops right up beside me.

I can't stand to see you so worried. She nuzzles her nose into the crook of my arm until I pick her up. *It's not like you.*

"Yes, well, I've never been forced to stare a murder in the face—quite literally. Someone killed the poor girl," I whisper, trying to make it look as if I were talking gently to my sweet cat. "Someone really wanted her gone. Maybe she knew something?"

"Who knew something?" a deep voice chides from behind, and I turn to find Sherlock bounding over and Jasper standing there with that obnoxious look on his face.

There she is. Bizzy Body Baker. Jasper's grin grows wider by the minute, and my mouth falls open at the audacity.

Fish hops into my lap a moment. *Oh, he's abhorrent.*

"You're telling me, sister," I hiss under my breath as she uses my shoulder as a springboard and takes off down the sand. I give Sherlock a quick scratch behind the ears. "Good morning, handsome."

Good morning, Bizzy. His inner voice is as deep in octave as his bark. *Where's my morning snack?* he teases as he cranes his neck past me. *Tell her to get back here. I've been craving kitten ears for the last two days.*

"Very funny." I hop to my feet. "Detective Wilder." I nod as I make my way past him. "Can I get a table for the two of you?"

"Yes, please. Here on the patio is fine."

"But it's so cold. We don't mind pets inside as long as they're leashed." I hitch my head toward the café, and soon enough they're seated inside at a table near the window. "Here's a menu," I say, pulling one off a nearby table. "And I'll be back to take your order shortly. Can Sherlock have a slice of bacon?"

"Yes." His cheek cinches, and I can't help but note how alarmingly handsome he looks. "In fact, I'll make it easy on you. I'll take the breakfast special."

"Perfect. I'll put your order in right away." No sooner do I get to the counter than Georgie walks in wearing a purple kaftan with silver threading woven throughout and smelling like—"Oh, dear. What is that smell?" I tuck my finger under my nose as I make my way around the counter.

Honestly? As management I should seriously consider giving her the boot for the safety of the other patrons' olfactory senses. In the least, she needs to sit out on the patio where the sea air has a shot of evicting that odor from her body.

"Let me guess"—I lift a finger—"my sister has been brewing something special in that cauldron of hers."

Georgie cackles as if it were true, and judging by the offensive odor, it might be. She lifts an arm and comes at me like she means it, her entire face brightening with pride. Her long hair cascades over her shoulders, but it's still a dicey call as to the source of those gray curls under her arms, and I'm not about to study them to see where they're sprouting from.

"You like?" She bats her lashes at me. "It's another patchouli deodorant Macy concocted. I let her know the first one didn't garner many fans, so I sent her back to the drawing board."

"Tell her strike two. It's back to the drawing board for her." I choke a moment on the offensive scent. "On second thought, tell her to burn the drawing board. If that's the best she can do, she might want to get out of that business before the fine people of Cider Cove run her out with torches and pitch forks."

"Oh hey, remember that guru friend I was telling you about? The one who lives in a yurt behind the dairy farm?"

"Yes," I say with caution as I quickly put in Jasper's order. I glance his way and our eyes lock a moment before he shoots his gaze out the window as if that were his intended ocular target all along. But it's too late. I caught him looking at me, red-handed, and a smile cinches over my lips.

I turn back to Georgie. "The guru friend who was going to look into my—predicament?" Every last fiber of my being silently prays that she doesn't blurt out the fact I have the ability to pry into other people's thoughts. But then Georgie does come up with twelve outlandish stories before lunchtime, which thankfully might work in my favor. It's safe to say, I find a strange comfort in the way the world perceives her quirkiness.

"Guess what?" Her blue-gray eyes widen the size of dinner platters. "He's heard of your predicament." She says that last word in air quotes.

I suck in a quick breath as I lean in. "Meaning?"

"Meaning he's familiar with your situation. He has a friend in Albany who swears he can do the same thing. He wants to talk to you. He says he'll be coming down this way next month. Don't you worry about a thing. I'll set the whole thing up."

"The guy from Albany?" A mild thread of alarm rails through me.

"No, silly. The guy with the yurt."

"Good Lord. I'm not interested. Look, Georgie, I know you mean well, but I'd rather you just forget I ever mentioned it. The last thing I want is to end up in a cage in some government lab. And, believe you me, that's exactly where they'll put me." I turn to look at Jasper. Thankfully, my gift isn't acting up today, and I actually have to work to steal a single thought.

Georgie follows my stare. "Ooh, I see the vampire is joining us for breakfast. Let me guess. He takes his blood warm."

"You're not far off. It turns out, he has a bite after all."

She swats me with a look of glee. "He bit you? Bizzy, this is big! You haven't had this kind of action since..." Her mouth hangs open as she struggles for words, and her fingers bounce off her thumb as if she were counting the years of my dry spell.

"Never you mind."

Jasper's order appears, and I quickly pick it up before heading back to the kitchen and tossing on a few extra strips of bacon.

It's Emmie's day off, and rumor—and all of her social media sites—has it that she's having breakfast with Grayson. Who knew a little investigative effort would yield a kernel of information for me and the rebirth of a relationship for her?

That about sums us up in a nutshell. When it comes to the two of us, Emmie always gets the better end of the romantic deal.

I speed back out, and Georgie salutes me from her seat in the corner where she, not-so-coincidentally, faces his direction.

Good luck, hot stuff. Georgie grins over at me. *Don't let him get away with not gifting you a nice big juicy bite on the neck. Aw, heck, take it on the kisser!*

I avert my eyes at the thought. Jasper and his ornery lips aren't getting anywhere near my kisser. *Not in this lifetime, buddy*, I say, looking right at him and my stomach bisects with heat at the thought of his lips falling to mine. How I hate that my body is such a traitor.

I zoom in his direction. "Your breakfast, coffee included—and a few extra strips of bacon for your sweet companion."

Sherlock pants away. *Thank you, Bizzy! Bacon, bacon!*

"I think he's thankful," I say, bending over and scratching him on the back. "You're welcome," I whisper.

A thought comes to me.

"Detective Wilder? Do you think I can ask you a quick question?"

He extends his hand in front of him. "Please, take a seat." There's a softness to him today, to his tone, to his demeanor, and a part of me wonders if it's some tried-and-true interrogation tactic that he's using on me.

It's no secret this man is after what I know. But, as it stands, the tables have turned, and now I'm after what he knows.

I land in the chair opposite him and get lost in those pale gray eyes without meaning to.

Beautiful. He frowns as if my so-called beauty offended him on some level. And with a man this ornery, it just might.

Yes, Detective Wilder is far too handsome for it to ever be fair, but he brings obnoxious to a whole new level.

"What's the question?" His lips twitch as if his ego is about to get stroked. He wishes.

I sigh as I lean forward. "Do you happen to know if Kaitlynn was wearing her engagement ring the night she was killed?"

His brows pinch at the center. There is a very virial manliness about Jasper that I can't quite explain. He has the face of a god, the body of an athlete, and the temperament of a starved crocodile.

"I don't know. Why? Did her stepsister mention it was missing?"

"No, nothing like that. I just wondered. You know, sometimes when I'm baking, I take my rings off. And I thought maybe she took hers off to wait tables that night. Maybe it was too big for her? Or maybe she thought it was too flashy."

She knows something. He's right back to glowering at me. *She knows something, and she's not telling me. The funny thing is, she thinks I won't be able to figure this out on my own.*

He thinks he's so smart.

"You know"—I clear my throat—"it's not like you won't be able to figure this out on your own." I come shy of winking and watch with hidden delight as his eyes grow twice their size. I couldn't help it. That's always been one of my favorite things to do—especially to people as arrogant as this.

He squints over at me while silently assessing me. "Figure what out? The engagement ring?"

"Yeah, I mean, all you'd have to do is make a call to the coroner's office, right?"

"Yes." He shakes his head as if contradicting himself. "What would it matter if she were wearing her engagement ring or not?" he says the words measured and slow as he narrows those alien eyes on mine. The dark peppering of stubble on his face makes them glow all the more. There's an unnecessary roughness about his demeanor, but he has an open face, and when paired with that all too stingy smile, he's perfectly affable. "Wait a minute." His lips expand as if to say he's got me. "You've got the ring, don't you?" His eyes run up and down my features frenetically as if quickly giving me an FBI worthy body analysis.

A hard sigh escapes me. I have never been a very good liar. Each time I've tried to get away with something, I've been magnificently called out on it—much like right now.

"All right, I have it," I snip. "But only because I happened to stumble upon it."

He leans in hard. "Bizzy, you have to hand that over right now."

"No."

"Yes." His eyes grow wide with disbelief. "I can charge you with tampering with evidence. I can haul you out of here in handcuffs if I want to."

I suck in a quick breath. "And to think, I gave you extra bacon."

"Bizzy Bizzy," a familiar deep voice chimes, and I turn to find my father heading this way with Macy in tow.

My father has called me Bizzy Bizzy for as long as I can remember, *remember*. He's where I get my dark hair and light eyes from. He's handsome, or so the long line of ladies that is always circling him has convinced us of it.

My father's grin widens a notch my way before his brows jump. Macy swats him and whisks him off to a seat.

"That's my father," I snip to the ornery detective. "And you may not drag me off in handcuffs in front of him. He is the sweetest man in the world. He's kind and nice and everybody likes him." I shake my head at the thought. "It's his superpower or something. Anyway, yes, I have her things. It was brought to my attention yesterday that they were still here. I need to get in touch with her mother—or her fiancé, Chris Davidson."

He closes his eyes a moment as if he's struggling to contain himself.

"Yes, Bizzy, I need to get in touch with the both of them again myself. But please do not go near either one of them. In a case like this, you never know who could be responsible for the carnage."

"Oh, come on"—I balk—"her own mother?"

"I've seen it," he spits it out so fast he doesn't skip a beat.

It takes everything in me to wrap my mind around something so gruesome.

"Okay"—I shudder—"but I met Chris that night. He'll warm up to me. I can ask him if he wants the engagement ring back. I mean, technically, it would go to him, right?"

"I don't know. I'm not well-versed in engagements." *Not that I didn't have the chance. But I made the right call. Every day I'm reminded of it.* His eyes sweep over my features. *Including this day.*

"Neither am I for the record."

"That's right. You skipped right to the wedding." His chest rumbles with a laugh.

Incoming ten o'clock. Georgie's voice comes in clear just as a shadow darkens the table, and we look up to

113

a sight of horror—my father grinning and holding out a hand toward Jasper.

"Nathaniel Baker. I'm Bizzy's father," he says it with a sly grin because he says everything with a sly grin. "I hear you're a vampire. Is that true?"

"Jasper Wilder." He shakes my father's hand. "Homicide detective. I think that technically makes me a vampire *hunter*. Care to join us?"

"No, no, your breakfast is getting cold. Just wanted to say hello." He looks my way with that ever-expanding grin on his face. "I hear you'll have a booth at the Harvest at the Cove deal. Congrats. Georgie is trying to get me to sponsor a booth for her." He slaps Jasper on the back. "Don't be like me and collect wives for a living. The wives leave and you'll get stuck with the mothers-in-law." He pretends to shoot him before heading back to the table where Georgie and my sister look as if they're taking bets on something—most likely the unhinging of my sanity.

"He's right," I say. "Your breakfast is growing cold. I'll see you around, detective."

"It's Jasper," he insists. ***Why won't she call me Jasper?***

"*Jasper*," I smart. I'm about to get up, but I lean in instead. "Where can I find Chris Davidson? And don't think I can't get this information on my own. I can google him, or I can go back to Sweet Cheeks and ask Rissa. Or I can—"

He's back to closing his eyes, but this time instead of a fit of frustration he seems to be acquiescing.

"What Ales You," he says. "It's his family's brewing company. They have a big plant just outside of—"

"Seaview." I nod. "I'm familiar. They have a restaurant and a bar on site. Emmie took me there for my twenty-first birthday."

His brow arches as if he were amused. "Did you enjoy it?"

"I don't drink, but the beer battered fish and chips were to die for." I wince. "Thank you," I say just under my breath. "Enjoy your breakfast." I stand to leave and he lifts a finger.

"One-thirty," he says. "I'll be taking a late lunch. I'll meet you there," he says it stern enough while locking eyes with me. *It's not like I'm going to stop her. Heck, she's already proven unstoppable. Not only do I have a homicide investigation that's going sideways, but I've got a wild card that's willing to put herself in harm's way while playing armchair detective.*

My mouth opens with surprise as I'm about to rip him a new one for even suggesting I'm an armchair anything, but I think better of it.

"Thank you, *Jasper*." I swallow down my pride. "I look forward to getting to know you better. And for the record, I just want to make sure Kaitlynn's things get into the right hands."

"They will. I'll be collecting them before I leave."

I narrow my gaze over his with marked hostility as I resist the very real urge to wrap my hands around his neck.

"I'll bring them to lunch with me."

He cinches his lips. *A woman who needs to have the last word. It's best to hand over the reins if you want any peace. I've learned that before the hard way. But those lips.*

I turn to leave and take my lips along with me.

9

Downtown Seaview is beautiful despite the fact the autumn air is frigid. The high-rises glitter like jewels in the afternoon sun. I take a turn to the outskirts of town where the What Ales You brewery sits like a robotic behemoth sprawled over acres of what looks to be the edge of the world. There is literally nothing behind it or near it for miles.

I park just out front and head into the cosmopolitan restaurant that was tacked onto the plant decades ago by the Davidson family. I still remember coming here with Emmie and our friends on my twenty-first birthday—Emmie's first but not last attempt to get me good and shnockered.

It didn't work.

As soon as I caught on that beer, and coincidentally all alcohol, tastes the way nail polish remover smells, I wanted nothing to do with the iconic rite of passage. And I've wanted nothing to do with liquor ever since either. I have nothing against it. I just don't want it.

Large gold letters sit against a polished black backdrop with the words *What Ales You Eatery* printed on the side of the building. I head on in through the heavy glass door, and the scent of French fries and beer hits my senses.

I'm insanely hungry. I'm also insanely *not thirsty* for beer, which is most likely a good thing since I'm probably a lightweight and I happen to have driven myself out this way. Not to mention I'll be alone with Jasper. Heaven knows I'll need ahold of every one of my senses to deal with him.

The waitress asks to seat me, and I tell her I'm meeting Jasper Wilder. Her eyes grow wide as she bears an all too approving grin. I follow her deep inside and straight to a table by the window where Jasper greets me with a short-lived smile.

He stands a moment as I take a seat. "Bizzy Baker. You ready for your first covert op?" He gives a slight wink, and I can't help but think he's mocking me.

She smells good. What is that? Lilacs? Gardenia? No, it's something warmer. Something that reminds me of home.

"It's vanilla," I say, giving a slight wink of my own right back, and he looks as if he's just seen a ghost. "You looked like you were wondering what that delicious scent was. I practically bathed in vanilla before I left. I was helping Emmie whip up another batch of apple walnut cinnamon rolls and accidently spilt the bottle of vanilla on my jeans. That about says everything you need to know about my talents in the kitchen. But I do wish I had them. Anyway, I'd change, but it'd be a waste of expensive perfume. If you knew how much a bottle of vanilla extract costs, you might actually faint."

He squints over at me a moment. "I think I know. My mother bakes. She's lamented about it a few times. And you were right. I was thinking that you smelled good. You're intuitive. I like that." He's right back to narrowing his gaze over me, and I bubble with a laugh.

There is nothing better than testing a grown man's sanity.

"A compliment." I perk up just enough. "Women appreciate that, and it's a surefire way to get on their good side. But I'm guessing you know exactly how to get on a woman's good side. *And* I'm guessing women like to get on your good side, too. I think it's safe to assume you're being chased by a fair share of women. And if not, you will be in Cider Cove. I witnessed Mayor Woods blatantly making a play for your attention."

A waitress comes by, and we quickly put in an order for a couple of fish and chips and drinks. Just water for me, but Jasper agrees to try the apple beer.

He tilts his head to the side. "So you're giving me dating tips? I like that." He pulls his lips into a line as he leans in over his elbows.

He's getting comfortable with me. Either that or he's setting me up. I still haven't figured out how to read him. One thing I can read loud and clear is the fact he's alarmingly attractive. It doesn't seem fair. My heart can't stop racing in his presence, and my stomach bottoms out in that annoying roller coaster way each time he bears those gray high beams he calls eyes into mine.

"So—are you dating?" I clear my throat. "I mean, they don't call Cider Cove, Lover's Cove for nothing." I can feel my face heat ten degrees. Lover's Cove? Did I really need to go there? A part of me thinks I did. "Has anyone in town caught your eye? Or are you an equal opportunity dispatcher of your carnal affections?" I'm guessing the latter.

His chest thumps with a silent laugh.

Yes, you've caught my eye. He nods my way as if he said the words out loud, and a breath catches in my throat.

"No one in particular." He shrugs, but his magnetic gaze never leaves mine, and I'm finding it impossible to look away. "How about you? Are you seeing anyone?"

"No. I've dated here and there, but I'm so busy with the inn—and my family, and Emmie and Georgie. I guess you can say I have a pretty full life."

"You should make time for yourself." He twirls his glass between his fingers as he looks my way. "Life has a way of slipping on by when we least expect it, and the next thing we know, years have danced by."

"If you're about to segue into a soliloquy about how my eggs won't last forever, you'll have to stand in line behind my mother. You're not about to ask for grandchildren, are you?" I can't help but tease him.

He grimaces just as our food arrives.

"I'm sorry." He holds up a hand. "In no way was I about to segue into that arena. I fully trust you can handle that on your own. How about we discuss the case?"

I dunk a piece of beer battered fish into the malt vinegar and die on the inside as I take a sinful bite. A hard moan comes from me, and something akin to white noise sizzles through Jasper's mind. I'm more than familiar with that high frequency whooshing sound because it just so happens to be the same response most men have to anything sexual. And that's one bit of telepathic info I'm sorry I'm privy to.

"It's just as good as I remember," I'm quick to assure him. "And yes, the case. Do we know if Chris is at the plant today? I think we should speak to him."

"He is." His left brow lifts high into his forehead. "But it will be me speaking to him. I'm sorry, Bizzy. You and I both know he might be the killer. I can't put you in that kind of danger."

"You said yourself it was a crime of passion. He's not killing me."

"He might if he thinks you're onto him."

"If that's the case, he might kill you, too."

He gives a solid blink as if his exasperation with me was growing. "He won't. I'm the investigating detective. Believe me when I say he will be on his best behavior in my presence."

"Ah-ha!" I'm quick to point my finger at him. "So, you agree that you'll get nothing from him but a big hoax of a personality. That's why you need me."

He leans in. "I don't need you, Bizzy."

My eyes widen at the audacity.

His mouth twists with disdain. *And why did that just feel like a lie?*

Ha! "You do need me and we both know it."

"No, I don't." He shakes his head emphatically. "Because the last thing I need is another homicide investigation on my hands. Trust me. I'm a very easygoing person."

"I've yet to see evidence of this."

He's right back to closing his eyes. "Okay. You may not see it in this instance, but I'm also protective of the people I care about."

"*Aw.*" I don't bother to hide my sarcastic inflection. "You've known me for five sweet seconds and already you're pulling the *I care about you* card."

"I care about you as a person. You're the innkeeper. You have a very important position. A lot of people are relying on you. You have a loving family."

"Let's not take things too far. They've been on their best behavior around you."

A soft smile bounces on his lips. "You have Fish. And she needs you. The last place anyone wants to see you in is the morgue."

A shiver runs through me.

"Fair enough." I give a quick glance around the vicinity. If Chris Davidson is here, then I predict I'm going to have an impromptu run-in with him very, very soon. Jasper can't hang around the brewery forever. Besides, Chris and I are practically old friends.

"I know what you're thinking." His serious, bordering on hateful stare never leaves his face. "You think I'll run off to the station soon enough and you'll have Chris all to yourself."

I gasp and hold my breath.

My goodness, he's just read my mind!

My goodness, what if *he* can read minds?

This is truly my worst nightmare, coming upon another version of myself in this cold and weary world and not having them disclose themselves to me. If he were just like me, the decent thing to do would be confess it—quickly.

I glare at him openly.

My, what big eyes you have. I lean in, trying to read his body for any kind of a reaction. ***What big ears you have.*** Again nothing. ***I bet you have a very big—***

His lips curl at the tips. "Bizzy?"

"Ah-ha!" I slam my hand down on the table. "I caught you."

He cocks his head to the side, seemingly confused. He's a darn good actor, I'll give him that. But, then again, I bet they teach you an acting skill or two in Detective 101.

"I was just going to say there's a woman who won't stop looking this way. I think I recognize her from the café this morning." He nods behind me, and I turn to find an all too familiar blonde who has me groaning with grief.

"Macy," I mutter under my breath as my sister breezes over in a tight crimson leather jacket paired with long matching boots that ride up over her knees. She gives a little wave and speeds this way as quick as a poltergeist—and, believe me, I'd welcome an entire army of the dead rather than have to deal with my sister right now.

"What a coinky dink." Macy presses her finger into her dimple and turns it like a key. She's always loved playing the ditz, but my surly sister is anything but.

"Macy"—I sigh—"this is Detective Wilder. He's working on the homicide investigation."

"Why hello, Detective Wilder. I believe I saw this exact same scenario playing out this morning at the inn." Her fingers do a little dance between us. "So, are the two of you—"

"*No*," we both say it in unison, and I look to him as my mouth falls open.

Jasper tosses a quick glance out the window as if he were growing tired of our non-relationship.

I stand quickly. "Would you please excuse us for a moment?" I grab ahold of Macy and haul her out to the back patio where the brisk fall air is ready to greet us. "Are you stalking me?"

Macy's bright red lips contort in every shape. "What, *you*? No. I'm actually stalking him." She turns back and waves to Jasper through the window. "Dad mentioned

125

something about lunch at this place and, truthfully, I was hoping it'd just be the two of us."

"Macy, I can't remember the last time we had lunch together."

She frowns as he turns back my way. "Not with you." She gives my cheek a little pinch. "But I do love you just the same. Now tell me. Are you bedding that hottie, or do I have to do it?"

"What?" I swat her on the arm. "Would you stop."

"I won't stop," she says it in her own sweet ironic way. "Bizzy, whether you like it or not, he's a hot commodity. All I'm saying is that we should keep it in the family, if you know what I mean. We have prime beef real estate, and there are many, many buyers looking to land themselves a choice piece of—"

"Okay, okay, okay." I bat my hands over my ears. "Fine, yes. I'm interested." But only in as much as to keep my sister's fangs out of my way. That side of beef and I have some serious business to contend with, and I don't need my sister mucking up the waters with her overripe ovaries. "He's mine," I say, glaring at him through the window, and he shoots me an equally dissatisfied look right back. "He's ornery, and mean, and controlling, but yes, he's mine." I blink over at my sister. "Hands off. Got it?"

She makes a face. "Fine. Have it your way. The next vampire that strolls into town belongs to me. And remember, the tall, dark, and brooding ones are usually better suited for yours truly." She glances his way. "Both in and out of the bedroom."

The nice thing about Macy is that she speaks her mind so much, there's very little left to read.

"Come here." She pulls me into a quick embrace, and that patchouli gone wrong olfactory offense hits me.

"Word to the deodorant making wise." I shake my head at her. "I'd buy an entirely new drawing board if I were you."

We head back in, and I wave my sister off as I resume my seat at the table, but Macy's stilettoed feet have stalled in the process of exiting.

"Goodbye, Detective Wilder." She pinches a wry smile, and I can feel it coming. "It seems my sister has informed me the two of you are indeed on your way to coupledom." My eyes spring wide. I'm one second from impressing the heck out of the detective next to me once he sees how efficiently I can carry out a homicide of my own. "Be nice to her. She's the *special* one in the family." She expands the sickly-sweet smile my way. "And no need to feel inhibited in the bedroom. Bizzy doesn't kiss and tell."

"Okay," I say, giving her a slight shove. "Oh, look, I think I see them towing your car away."

She waves me off. "Have fun. Call me!" she shouts as she makes her way out the door.

I turn to face Jasper. "Before you say a word, or gloat, or vomit, I just want to add that I was forced to tell her those things or she would have meddled in our investigation."

His cheek glides up one side, and my heart begins with that erratic thumping again. Dear Lord. At this point I'd be fine with it imploding. Every part of my body feels like a traitor around this man.

"Don't worry." A smile blinks over his face. "I won't blow your cover. And you're right. She won't interfere in the investigation and neither will you." He nods to my plate. "Your food is getting cold."

"So is my heart." I spot a tall man with a heavy tan heading this way, chatting it up with the patrons as he makes his way over, and my mouth falls open.

"How's everything here? You enjoying the food?" He's wearing an ear-to-ear grin. His hair looks a bit blonder than it did the night of the bonfire, but it's him. It's Chris Davidson in the flesh.

"Everything is great," I say and I can see Jasper shaking his head ever so slightly my way. "You don't remember me, do you?"

He inches back and does a double take at Jasper. "No, but I remember you, Detective Wilder. What brings you here? Did they find the killer?" His eyes widen a notch, and he looks genuinely concerned.

"No." Jasper smacks his lips my way. "I was just bringing my girlfriend in for a quick bite. I hear it's the best place to eat near the station."

Something warms in me when he refers to me as his girlfriend, and I suddenly hate that part of myself.

Chris bucks with a laugh and slaps Jasper on the back. "I can't contest that." He squints my way. "Hey, I think you do look familiar. But I can't seem to place you."

"We met the night of the bonfire." I shrug. Guilty as charged.

The smile glides right off his face. "That's right. You were talking to Rissa." He takes a deep breath. "Kaitlynn was my life. It's been real hell without her. All I can do is plaster a fake smile on my face to get through my shift here. And then I go home and stare at the pictures I have of the two of us. Whoever did this to her didn't just kill Kaitlynn. They killed our future, our future family. Everything is gone, and nothing will ever be the same."

Jasper's chest expands. "I'm sorry, Chris. I can promise you, I'm doing everything I can to catch the killer."

"Do it faster." He looks my way. "What was Sammy telling you that night?"

"Sammy?"

"Sammy Walton. She was the brunette next to you and Rissa."

"Oh?" The girl who was hugging Sherlock comes to mind. "She was infatuated with my dog. His dog actually."

Chris nods as if he understood. "She's a big animal lover. I can see her doing that. All right. Your meal is on me." He looks to Jasper. "If you discover anything, anything at all, call me, find me. I don't care what time it is. I want to be in the loop."

He backs up, and I'm filled with panic at the thought of him slipping away without having enough time to interrogate him properly.

"Oh, Chris," I say and Jasper is right back to blinking hard. "I just want you to know that Rissa mentioned Kaitlynn's cosmetics line to me, and I've agreed to sell it at the inn as sort of a tribute to her."

His lips purse as if this didn't please him on some level. "That's very kind of you. I'll stop by some time and check it out. I know she would have gotten a kick out of that. Take care." He speeds off without bothering to stop off at any more tables.

"So? What did you think?" I lean in, my gaze still set on Chris until he disappears down a darkened hall.

"I think you're smooth, and crafty, and far too dangerous to bring along on any more adventures." Jasper hooks my gaze with his own. "I'm assuming you've already spoken to Jeannie Branch."

"You'd be wrong. You know what they say. If you assume, you just might make an *ass* of *u* and *me*."

A thunderous laugh bounces through his chest. "Oh, sweetie, you've already done that."

"Don't you call me sweetie."

"Why not?" His brows rise as if he were amused. "You told your sister we're dating."

"If we were dating, you'd call me something far more endearing."

"Like Killer Bait?"

I suck in a quick breath. "I am not putting myself out there as bait for some killer."

"So you think." He leans in. "Listen to me, Bizzy Baker, and listen well—because this will be my final warning. Do not stick your nose into my investigation. I'll reach out to Jeannie for you. She's the next person on my list."

"I thought you already questioned all of the suspects?"

"Briefly. But the investigation is ongoing."

"Don't do me any favors. I'll be talking to Jeannie myself. Stay out of my business affairs. I've got a spa to stock in remembrance of Kaitlynn Zimmerman. One of us actually knew her. One of us actually cares enough to do anything to find her killer."

And that's exactly what I'm afraid of. He tilts his head my way.

"I'll see you back at the inn." I rise to leave and collect my purse.

"You didn't finish your meal."

"I've lost my appetite." I take off back into the icy autumn afternoon and take in a lungful of air—a pleasure Kaitlynn will never have again.

And I'm determined to make sure the killer won't enjoy the pleasures of the free world for too much longer either.

I glance back at the eatery, only to find Jasper standing outside the establishment with his hands buried in his pockets as he watches me from behind.

Our eyes lock for a moment before we both turn our separate ways.

Call me sweetie, indeed.

No sooner do I get back to the Country Cottage Inn than I notice a text message on my phone.

Hey, Bizzy, it's me, Jasper. I hope you don't mind. Fish gave me your number this morning. I pause to roll my eyes. It's true. Fish wears my number around her neck and can freely give it to anyone. **Just spoke to the coroner. Kaitlynn had her engagement ring on at the time of the murder. Just thought you might want to know. It seems you left before you could give me her things. Please don't tamper with them. I'll collect them soon.**

Kaitlynn was wearing her engagement ring.

Huh.

That ring in her purse must be a cocktail ring then. Whatever it is, I'm certain it's a serious piece of jewelry. Maybe she was about to hock it to help with her new business? Rissa said she borrowed money from her mother. Maybe she needed more.

I'll have to surrender her belongings to Jasper. That much is true.

But not before I have one more look at everything.

10

True to his word, or his threat as it were, Jasper showed up at around seven and asked for Kaitlynn's belongings. I shoved the bag at him without a peep of protest. The fact is, I didn't need to protest. I meticulously took each item out and took a picture of them with my phone. I wore gloves the second time around to rifle through her purse. Not sure why, but it felt like the official thing to do before the big surrender.

Jim, the mailman, strides over to the front desk of the inn with his perennial cheery grin. We're always the first on his route, so we get our mail early.

"Top of the morning to ya!" He drops the mail into the bucket behind the counter as he's done a hundred times before.

"Right back at you, Jim."

He mock salutes me as he heads on out. ***Pleasant lady. Simply the best.***

I smile as I hear it. Jim has had that same thought about me each and every time he sees me—and since it's not bad nor marred with innuendo, I don't mind one bit.

Jasper didn't come in for breakfast this morning. I spotted his truck speeding away with Sherlock in the passenger's seat just as I was leaving to head to the inn.

All right, so I felt bad how we left things. I don't know why that is, but it's true. I swipe the mail from the bucket and quickly sift through it, putting the important bills to the right and dumping the plethora of ads and realtor notices promptly into the trash. There's a handful of letters for our guests, and I file those into their proper slots.

It's Nessa's job to deliver them to the guests' suites, but I always try to make things easy on her by organizing them by room number.

Emmie sweeps by from the café and gives a quick wave as she heads for the door.

"Whoa, whoa! Where are you headed? The café is that way," I tease. I've got a sinking feeling I'm not going to like her answer.

Here we go. She flashes that killer smile my way.

"Would you believe I feel a horrible bout of the flu coming on?"

"No. Try again." I wince over at her. "This time with the truth."

"Fine." She cinches her purse over her shoulder as she speeds my way. Her dark curly hair bounces over her shoulder in coiled springs. "Before I get to the good part, I want you to know I came in extra early and made up all the croissants, apple walnut cinnamon rolls, and Danishes anyone could want. I made sure all the cookies and brownies were well-stocked, and I've already put in the weekly order so you won't have to do it. We have two extra staff on top of our regular staff manning the fort, and I know how much you hate our labor to be on the uptick, so I'm taking one for the team and taking the day off."

"Good. Because as soon as Nessa and Grady show up, you and I will head over to see Jeannie Branch to place an order for Natural Beauty products so we can stock up the spa."

Her lips crimp with disappointment. "I'm sorry to break it to you, Biz, but I can't go. I told Grayson I'd go with him to the orchard this morning. We're going on an apple picking date."

"Can't you reschedule?"

"No can do. His boss at Sweet Cheeks wants only the freshest ingredients, and he's in charge of bringing in a bushel this afternoon. I promised I'd help. Besides"—her head bobbles from side to side—"we crested second base on our last date. I think this is going to happen for us this time."

"It happened for you last time. Remember? And then it ended badly."

"It didn't end badly. He forgot to call. Over and over again." She wrinkles her nose. "Try not to rain on my apple picking parade, would you?"

"Fine, go pick some apples. Pick up a bushel for the Cottage Café while you're at it, and I'll pay you for your time."

"Whoo-hoo!" she cheers as she heads for the door. "It's nice to have your bestie as your boss." She turns around. "Oh, and Bizzy? Don't go see that woman alone. The last thing I want is some maniac offing you."

"You sound a lot like Jasper."

"Ooh. *Jasper.*" She wiggles her shoulders. "I think you just like to say his name."

She takes off just as Nessa and Grady arrive. And they both generously agree to keep watch over the inn for me. And since I'm down one bestie, refuse to bring along my psycho of a sister, and my brother the legal eagle is out of the question, I head to the only person I can turn to at a time like this.

Georgie's cottage sits all by its lonesome, even though it's closest to the inn itself but still far enough away for it to feel like a tiny piece of paradise. Her studio cottage is situated on a grassy knoll and has a premium view of the cove. The water looks steely gray today, there's a marine layer lying over the ocean, and the air is both crisp and briny.

No sooner do I come upon Georgie's quaint little cottage than the familiar sound of breaking glass slices through the silence. I'd be alarmed if I wasn't used to it by now. Georgie spends her days walking up and down all the beaches of Maine looking for abandoned bottles she can turn into art.

I give a brisk knock over the door, and soon enough the sound of chaos dies down in there. I can hear her footfalls headed in this direction, and the door opens, revealing that pleased-to-see-me smile she wears for just about everyone. Her hair is curly yet frizzy as can be, framing her face like a salt and pepper mane. She's dressed in denim overalls covered with paint, and there's a strong chemical odor emitting from her cottage.

Her entire being brightens at the sight of me.

"Well, look who it is, the vampire queen. Come in, come in! I want to hear all about it. Is he a good kisser? Does he bite?" She presses out each word with a greedy grin.

"I'll come in, but for the sake of both our lungs, we should probably keep the door open." I wave my hand over my nose as I stride inside. Georgie has the place covered in large pieces of plywood in which she's glued amazing mosaic patterns. On her work table there are dozens of vases and an oval mirror encrusted in what looks like jade sea glass. "Oh, Georgie, this is gorgeous! You're going to be a hit at the Harvest at the Cove event. I can't wait to see everyone clawing to get your things."

"I know, I know. I'm so excited." She trots to the kitchenette and comes back with two shot glasses filled with wheatgrass. "Time to energize your day."

"Thank you," I say, knocking mine back quickly. I've had enough of them to know what they are. And she's right. They really do energize my day. I shudder once the aftertaste hits me. "You added the lime like I suggested. I love it!"

"Just for you, my sweets. I don't do bitters."

"For all the care you take of yourself, you'd think you'd ventilate this place. You're going to get high off all the fumes."

She looks at me from under her lashes with a note of mischief in her eyes. "That's what I'm counting on. Now onto the details." She motions for me to hurry. "Spill, spill!"

"We haven't kissed. And before you ask, we *won't* be kissing."

"What?" She looks crestfallen at the news. "When Macy got back to Lather and Light, she clearly said the two of you were dating. Back in my day, that was code for doing it."

"Well, that's not happening either." A brief, heated vision of the two of us in the throes of passion flits through my mind, and I quickly wave it right back out. "Anyway, that's not why I'm here. What are you doing in about a half an hour?"

She squints hard as she folds her arms across her chest. "Anything you want me to do."

"Perfect. We're about to go on a shopping spree."

And who knows?

We might just bag a killer.

The alcove of homes that lies directly adjacent to the entry of the orchard has always been ritzy, extremely expensive, and highly sought-after. Before my parents divorced, we lived in Seaside Plains, about a six-mile drive up the way in a comfortable split-level home that was indeed split down the financial middle once my parents were forced to sell in the aftermath of their maritial dissolution.

My brother was already in college by then, and my mother bought a small condo near the beach where my sister and I lived with her for a time. My father was busy dotting all of Cider Cove with new residences and wives, neither of which lasted long enough to provide any stability.

I called Jeannie early this morning to let her know that the inn was looking to buy up some inventory for the spa in honor of Kaitlynn, and she sounded perfectly relieved to hear it.

Georgie and I pull up to the house number Jeannie gave me, and I spot the double wide garage door open, so we park and head on up.

The overstuffed garage is brimming with brown boxes. Stacks taller than I am line either side of it, and more boxes eat up the middle. A perky blonde with wet spaghetti-like hair beams with a smile as she heads over to meet us. Her skin looks pasty in the sun, and her nose and cheeks are dotted with freckles.

"You must be Jeannie," I say, extending a hand her way and she gives it a healthy shake.

"That I am. And you must be the woman Kaitlynn sent to save me. I'm drowning in potions and lotions. My dad said he'd pay you to take it all off my hands." She rolls her eyes. "He was teasing, of course." *Not really, but that's for me to know.*

A warm laugh bounces out of me. "I'll do my best to help you out. This is my friend, Georgie."

Georgie extends her hand as well. "I'm a buyer for Lather and Light." *Oh, she's not the killer, Bizzy. I can just tell by that sweet look in her eyes. I'll let you know when we come upon the monster that did this.*

Great.

I grimace over at her. And if Macy didn't already despise her career choices, she'll have a conniption once Georgie shows up with a truckload of product.

"Wow! Lather and Light? I love that place. This is fantastic." Jeannie is quick to lead us up to the garage with a newfound enthusiasm. And before we know it, she has at least sixteen boxes opened at our feet and we carefully curate what we think would work best for the spa. Correction, Jeannie and I carefully curate what we think would be best for the spa while Georgie takes a Sharpie and marks every box she'll take—and by the looks of things, she's taking them all. My sister will be steaming when she sees brand new inventory showed up uninvited. I'd intervene, but I'm pretty sure this can be slotted under payback for that little stunt she pulled at the brewery.

"Hey, Jeannie? If all that stock doesn't work out for Lather and Light, would you take returns?"

"Not a problem. Once it leaves the garage, at least there's the illusion of hope that it won't be coming back."

And I pray it doesn't come back.

Georgie turns around. "Hey, Jeannie Bo Beanie!" Good grief. She's already gifted her a cheery moniker. "How about those boxes?" She points to the top shelf on the right.

"No, sorry, Georgie!" *Heck no.* "Those are my private reserves."

"Gotcha!" She offers us a double thumbs-up.

Heck no? They must have something in them other than cosmetics? Or maybe a premium blend she's slow to part with?

The address label on one of the boxes catches my eye. It's addressed to Bowden Development. I glance at a few more boxes and note they're all the same.

I tap my finger on one. "What's Bowden Development? Is that some sort of an umbrella corporation?" No sooner do I get the words out than I regret them. I just gave her an easy out if it were a cover-up.

Jeannie turns my way, still panting from reorganizing all of the inventory for our sakes.

"It's my dad's development company." She wrinkles her nose. "Contrary to what people believe, I don't have a trust fund. My dad kicked in my portion of the start-up. So you can see why he was so happy when he heard you were on your way." She makes a face. "He'll get paid back eventually, though. I can't thank you enough, Bizzy. I'll stop by the café sometime and see how it's selling if you don't mind. I'm still in this. I'm not quitting Natural Beauty, but I think Kaitlynn and I got in a little over our heads. Once I regroup and get the website working how it should, I think we'll—I'll be killing it." She cringes. "Horrible choice of words, I know."

I cringe along with her. "So, who do you think could have done such a thing? Such a violent crime."

"I don't know." Jeannie's eyes flutter, and for a brief moment I think she's about to pass out. "I hate thinking about it. She and Chris had their problems, but he's not a killer. And I know that the sheriff's report said that she and Rissa were seen arguing before she died, but I don't know. Rissa would argue with Kaitlynn about anything. She still blames Kaitlynn's father for breaking up her parents." She shrugs. "I spoke to the detective that night. Wow, was he hot." She's back to wincing, and this time I do my best not to roll my eyes. "And I only say so because I know Kaitlynn would agree with me. Not that we had the same taste in men." She sticks her tongue out as if she were about to be sick.

"You don't care for Chris?"

"Chris is okay. It was the other one."

"What other one?" I try to maintain my composure.

"Well, I guess if you count Cameron, there were a few other ones. But no matter what anyone says, Cameron was truly Kaitlynn's best friend. They dated briefly in high school, but they became closer after their split."

"Huh. I wonder why she didn't stay with him? I mean, if they get along so well. You would think being with your best friend would be ideal."

"It would, but Cameron has a dark side that he apparently saves for his official plus one. She couldn't tolerate it. And, believe me when I say, not a lot of people can tolerate Cameron Weiss."

"Oh right. They don't call him the *Weiss* Guy for nothing," I say, thinking quick on my feet.

"Ha! That's funny! And you're right. He is a wise guy." *Among other, far more sinister things. But then, Kaitlynn did have a hankering for the sinister and the secretive.*

Secretive?

"Does he still work down at the wharf in Rose Glen?" I have no clue where he works, or who he is, but I'm riding this wave of deception until I hit sand or wipeout.

"What? No, Cameron would never be caught slumming at the wharf. He was a Ward boy. They're prone to be difficult. Sorry if you went there."

A genuine laugh bounces through me. "I went to Dexter University. And believe me, I know all about those Ward boys and how difficult they can be." Jasper and that obnoxious ego bounces through my mind.

"Cameron is teaching classes at the community college in Rose Glen. That's probably where you got the wharf thing."

"Probably," I say.

"He's a guidance counselor, too."

"A guidance counselor." I know for a fact guidance counselors have drop-in hours, and I fully plan to utilize that to my advantage.

Georgie dances her way out of the garage as if she just won the lottery.

"I'll take it all, missy! Sold, sold, and sold!"

Jeannie and I share a warm laugh.

She looks to Georgie. "I'll have all the boxes you marked shipped to the Lather and Light by later this afternoon." She turns my way. "And if you want, I can help you get most of the stuff for the spa in the trunk of your car."

"That would be great. Hey, Jeannie? How did you and Kaitlynn meet?"

She winces. "We met at a party. I was new in town, and she was kind enough to show me around."

She helps load the boxes into my trunk and the entire time I try my hardest to get a bead on her thoughts, but she's too focused on the task at hand.

We thank Jeannie for her time and take off. I'm not entirely sure Jeannie is off my suspect list. Not that she gave me a reason to be suspicious, but I'm assuming killers rarely do.

Now to find Cameron Weiss and find out why a nice girl like Kaitlynn couldn't tolerate him.

11

Why is there a crap ton of Natural Beauty cosmetics in my stockroom? And by the way, I don't have a stockroom. It's called a *showroom*. And thanks to this petty prank you're pulling, I don't have customers either. Get down here and help me chuck this junk into the nearest body of water.

I can't help but giggle as I read Macy's text. She was astute as a child, and she's far shrewder than that as a wily adult. She's as adorable as she is mean, but that's just one of her loveable quirks.

I text back. **I can't help you. I'm at Rose Glen Community College. The new stock is a gift from Georgie. And it's not considered green to chuck**

things into a body of water. Sell it. W
You might even turn a profit for once.

My phone pings again. **Funny. Hey? Does what's-his-face have a brother? Because I would totally settle for a good-looking sibling of the male persuasion. Just letting you know.**

A dull laugh catches in my throat as I look up at the elongated sign sprawled across a concrete wall. *Rose Glen Community College, Where Dreams Become a Reality.*

I've always loved Rose Glen. Much like Cider Cove, Rose Glen is a small seaside community. But Rose Glen is far more of a fishing town than Cider Cove will ever be. They have a harbor and a huge wharf that features great places to eat, and tons of shops that are mostly geared toward tourists. But every now and again, I peruse the boutiques just to see what's new in the fashion world. If I ever needed to buy a dress for a special occasion, I've gone to the wharf with my credit card at the ready.

But I'm not shopping or visiting the wharf. I'm heading over to a drop-in counseling session with a man by the name of Cameron Weiss—Professor Weiss to be exact.

My phone pings again with another text from Macy.

Oh, and before I forget—I promise retribution for siccing Georgie on me. If I were you, I'd watch my cute little back.

Goodness.

I turn off the volume to my phone and bury it deep into my purse as I head into the brown brick structure. It's bright inside, and the nostalgic scent of academia clings in the air as I head down to the administrative end of the building. I'm more than familiar with RGCC since I spent two years here before transferring out to Dexter University. I can't believe that was years ago. It really does feel like just yesterday I was a nervous high school grad bearing notebooks with giant neon kiss prints over them and pens in a rainbow of colors. I was as comical to look at as I was studious.

A smattering of students sit at the open lounge as I sign in to see Professor Weiss, and I'm happy to note that there's not a student in line ahead of me. Before I can take a seat, the secretary, an older woman with droopy jowls and glasses that hang off a chain, cranes her neck my way as she shouts my name as if she didn't just see me jot it down.

"I'm here." I raise my hand a smidge. "That's me, Bizzy Baker."

She looks markedly annoyed as if my name somehow offended her. And she wouldn't be the first. My mother got a lot of flak for letting me run around with a nickname my sister gave me rather than the perfectly good moniker she gifted me.

I'm led to the first door that's opened in the back, and a nice looking man with a startlingly familiar face smiles up at me from his desk.

"Come on in," he offers. "I'm Cameron Weiss—just Cameron is fine. Feel free to shut the door if you like."

And I do just that. The office is small and boxy, and I spot a framed picture of him and Kaitlynn holding one another in front of a giant roller coaster, looking very much like a couple.

Cameron Weiss looks almost identical to Chris Davidson, same light brown hair, same light eyes, same everything, save for the golden tan. Cameron looks a wee bit heavier, but that extra cushioning gives him an overall softer appeal.

He flashes an easy smile my way. "So what can I do for you?" He leans back in his seat, and his leather chair begins to rock.

"I'm actually—um, looking into some classes for my niece. She's in her senior year, and I wanted to know what steps she'll need to take to enroll." Lies, all lies, but I'm half-afraid he'll look me up in their files and see that I've already moved on from this fine institution. And, sadly, the lies came all too easily.

"Sounds good. Enrollment is easy. Just have her pull up an application on the school's website, and"—he reaches back and pulls out a bloated pamphlet—"give her this. It includes days and hours for the placement test she'll need to take. And after that, have her see me."

"Oh, that's great." I bite my lip hard. That went far too quickly. Now what? I glance to the picture of the two of them once again. "Oh wow, I know her. I mean, I knew her." That last part comes out in less than a whisper.

Cameron takes a deep breath as he pulls the picture in close and studies it pensively.

"Kaitlynn," he finally manages. "She was everything to me." His chest bucks, and suddenly I feel like I want to be anywhere but here. Jasper is right. I shouldn't be doing this. And now look? I'm about to reduce a grown man to tears. He sniffs hard and seemingly regains his composure. "How did you know her?"

"Oh, she worked at the café at the inn I manage." I stop shy of telling him it was me who found her. "It's just horrible what happened."

"It's worse than that." He shakes his head. "So, you really knew her. Were the two of you—you know—friends?"

"We were a little more than acquaintances. But we were friendly. Kaitlynn was an angel to everyone—ornery customers included." Jasper comes to mind. Speaking of minds, I try my hardest to pry into the mind of the man in front of me, but he seems to be full of white noise—and it doesn't seem to be of the sexual variety either. I'm not sure what that means, but it might be his grief throwing off the signal.

"I see." He glides the picture back to its proper position.

"And how about you?" My hand presses to my chest in a fit of faux surprise. "Were you her fiancé? She always had such nice things to say about you." Another lie. And, yet again, I had no problem doing so. I hope at the end of the investigative day, I don't discover I'm a sociopath at heart.

Come to think of it, I don't ever remember Kaitlynn bringing up her fiancé.

"No, nothing like that. We were just good friends. I mean, we dated way back when." He nods to the picture. "But we've since moved on."

Cameron sighs heavily. "Kaitlynn was my very best friend. She was basically my other half. I loved her deeply—still do. But the fiancé you mention came by and swept her off her feet, and they were well on their way to getting married. I don't know what happened. They seemed to get along great, and the next thing I know they're on the rocks and less than a day later she's dead." He glares at the wall behind me a moment. "Brutally stabbed. You wouldn't even do that to an animal," he growls the words out as if he were talking to himself.

"I agree," I say quietly. "Did you say Kaitlynn and her fiancé were on the rocks?" I shake my head as if refuting the idea.

"That's right. Kaitlynn came by my house the night before, and she let me know she was finished with him."

"What?" I squawk, nearly falling out of my seat. "But this is the first I'm hearing of this." My mouth falls open as he looks to me as if he were puzzled by my reaction. "She was raving about him just that evening. I just figured everything was great between them. I guess I was wrong."

"A lot of people were wrong. I was thrilled about it. I thought maybe I'd have another shot with her, but that didn't work out. If you don't mind, I would appreciate it if you didn't say anything."

"Absolutely," I'm quick to let him know. "Especially since Kaitlynn probably never had a chance to tell him herself."

His chest rises and falls with a dull laugh.

"What?" A breath hitches in my throat. "Oh my goodness, you think he did it."

"Who else did it?" He ticks his head to the side as if it were obvious. "I'm sure it's a matter of days before the deputies arrest him. I'd kill him myself, but the idiot's not worth rotting in prison over."

"No, he's not." I shake my head frenetically. "Cameron, if you really feel sure about this, you need to tip off the sheriff's department yourself."

"No can do." His eyes widen a notch as if he were certain of it. "Chris Davidson, her fiancé, comes from a powerful family. It wouldn't surprise me if they twisted this somehow and made it look like it was me who did it. And believe me, they're crooked enough to drum up an entire army of witnesses who would vouch for the fact they saw me do it. Nope. I'm letting the homicide detectives work this one over. Chris might look as if he's got a good head on his shoulders, but he's not the brightest bulb. They'll find something. And I'm going to sit back and watch the entire Davidson clan implode like a crushed beer can."

My chest thumps as he lets the brewery pun fly.

"I didn't realize that. I'm sure waiting for the homicide detective to piece this together is really hard for you. Have you thought of leaving an anonymous tip?"

"There's nothing anonymous these days. Can't take the risk." His lips twitch my way. "But if you wanted to, I won't stop you."

A part of me wonders if I'm being manipulated right now.

His eyes grow red and teary as he pulls her picture forward again.

"Were you there that night?" I ask just above a whisper. "The night she was killed?"

He shakes his head. "I was on my way—took one look at the parking lot at the inn and knew it would be useless. I drove all up and down Main Street looking for a spot and I found nothing, so I turned back and came home. And once I got there, I got the news."

"I'm sorry. How did you find out? The television?"

"A friend texted." He looks out the window a moment just as a knock erupts at the door. "I'm sorry. I'm going to have to wrap this up. My secretary likes to keep me on track. I'm not allotted more than fifteen minutes per drop-in. Have your niece come by soon. I'll help her register for all the classes she needs."

"Thank you," I say as I rise out of my seat. "I know she'll appreciate that." I head for the door.

"I didn't get your name."

A small part of me screams *don't tell him the truth*. But he already knows where I work and what position I hold, and I did sign in after all.

"Bizzy Baker. It was nice to meet you."

I head back out into the crisp fall day and make my way to the parking lot, only to gasp once I see the sight before me.

Leaning against my car with his arms folded tightly, his lips pursed in what looks to be anger is a smoldering Detective Jasper Wilder.

"Are you following me?"

His eyes harden over me with a hint of disbelief tucked in each one. "Bizzy, I saw your car in the lot."

"Detective"—I lift my chin a notch as I unlock the car—"I believe you're in my way."

A dull chuckle bounces through him, his eyes still serious as stone over mine.

"I believe you are in *my* way." He tilts his head to the side. "So, what did you glean?"

"Wouldn't you love to know." I do my best to swat him away from the driver's side door, but he doesn't budge. "If you don't move, I'm going to think you like the beating."

His lips twitch upward as if he approved.

"Knew it," I hiss. "You're nothing but a pervert. You're very good at pretending to be on the right side of the law."

"And you're very good at pretending to be a homicide investigator. But you see, you are not. You are messing around in my investigation at every turn, tainting every single one of my suspects. You have no idea the amount of damage you could have caused to the case already. Trying to apprehend a killer is a very delicate dance."

"Well, Detective Wilder"—I narrow my gaze over his until he voluntarily steps over a notch—"I don't need you to invite me to the dance. Kaitlynn did that for me." I hop into the driver's seat and start up the engine. "And if I were you, I'd move my feet a little faster. I just got enough clues to shut down a half dozen homicide cases. The killer just might be closer than you think."

"And who would that be?" His silver eyes shine as bright as the sun, and they cause me to squint. His chest expands and he's oozing testosterone without even trying. My stomach bisects with heat at the sight of him.

"Sorry, detective, but my dance card is filled," I say as I start to speed off.

"Clear it," he bellows after me. "I'm coming by tonight."

Did he just say he's coming by tonight?

My stomach bisects with heat once again as if to say *I sure hope so*.

But I don't hope so.

I've never met a more obnoxious man in my life.

And I sure as heck don't care to tango with this one.

12

Okay, I confess.

I've primped and prepped and cleaned my cottage—not that Detective Wilder will be permitted beyond the front door but, in the event he decides to snoop and crane his neck over my shoulder, I've made provisions.

I check my look in the mirror. I may have changed my outfit—exactly four times. But I swear on all that is holy, it has nothing to do with that hard-nosed detective and everything to do with the fact a storm is rolling in. I settled on a yellow rain jacket and matching boots.

No, no, no, that's not right.

I quickly abandon the jacket and jump in a circle until I've freed my feet from the rubber contraptions. No reason to look like an homage to Morton Salt. Instead, I don a navy pea coat and a pair of slouchy black boots.

"That's better," I say, angling in the mirror. "I think."

Fish jumps up onto the sofa table and yowls at me.

"What is it, sweet girl?" I ask, leaning in and dropping a kiss right over her forehead.

Why are you wrecking the house? And more importantly, please tell me this exercise in frustration has nothing to do with that testy man and his dog. I've about had it with that wily pooch. Do you realize he captured me in his mouth as if I were a toy? That's what he does. He pins me down and pretends to bite me.

A quick visual of Jasper doing the same to me flits through my mind.

"You can't blame Sherlock. His father is a vampire. I bet he's seen him do it a thousand times before—to a thousand ready and willing women."

I'm not blind. I can see how attractive he is. And apparently, so can everyone else. I don't know why I've put so much effort into my appearance tonight. I haven't exactly had any luck with men in general. Not that I'm looking to get lucky. The few men I did date all came with rather active imaginations and entire streams of consciousness I wish I couldn't pry into.

One told me he was a CEO, only come to find out he was thinking about how thrilled he was that I would never find out he worked at a convenience store in Edison. Then there was an entire slew of guys who had their minds fixated on other women—not to mention the ones whose intentions were less than pure with me. Despite the fact they talked a good game, their thoughts were on another sleazy level. My so-called gift has always landed my boyfriends in hot water sooner or later. But the romantic in me would like to believe that there is one person out there for me—someone who wouldn't dream of thinking about other women, or lying to my face about anything. A part of me wonders if I'm asking too much. We are all humans after all, and Lord knows my thoughts aren't always the best. But there has to be a soulmate, a special someone out there for me somewhere—doesn't there?

A quick knock erupts over the door and I jump three feet, prompting poor Fish onto all fours with her back arched, fur standing on end, yowling in fear as if she were down nine lives.

I head over and pull it open as the wind presses the door back, and it could very well knock me down like a feather.

Jasper stands there with his dark hair slicked back and those silver eyes as mesmerizing as mercury. Gone is the suit, and in its place is a tweed jacket and dark jeans—a bouquet of sunflowers pressed in my direction and I gasp at the sight.

She is stunning. His eyes widen as the thought flits through his mind, and my cheeks heat upon hearing it.

"A peace offering." A humble smile graces his lips for less than a second as Sherlock jumps and does his best to bounce inside and catch himself a Fish.

"They're beautiful, and so unexpected," I say, carefully taking them from him. "Thank you, Detective Wilder—um, Jasper. If your plan was to catch me off guard, you've succeeded." I nod for him to come in, and now I'm thankful to heaven I excavated that pile of laundry off the sofa and powered my way through the mountain of dishes.

"You're welcome. And something tells me it's not easy to catch you off guard," he says just as Sherlock works his way out of his collar and bolts like lightning onto the couch, onto the sofa table, down the hall, and through both bedrooms and back as he chases Fish around in a blur.

"Fish!" I cry.

"Sherlock!" Jasper bellows.

Both Jasper and I shout at the two of them at top volume, and it only adds to the general chaos.

Jasper covers the walkway that leads to the hall with his legs at a wide stance, his arms dangling below just as Fish dives between them and he does his best to catch Sherlock but to no avail.

"I'll get her!" I shout as I crouch in front of him. And sure enough, Fish bolts right for me, using my chest as a springboard and knocking me right onto my back as effective as a freight train. "*Geez!*"

No sooner do I catch my breath than Sherlock zooms between Jasper's legs, and in a desperate attempt to grab him, Jasper grasps him by the tail, pulling him forward until he falls over me like a building.

A shrill scream evicts from my throat, and I squeeze my eyes shut tight just as his body comes crashing within an inch of mine.

I pry my eyes open slowly, only to find those steel gray eyes staring back at me.

"Hello," he grunts and his breath holds the scent of fresh mint. My gaze drifts to his mouth as if he just threw out an invitation.

Oh dear, Bizzy! Fish roars along with the thought. *He's going to bite you, isn't he?*

I'm not that lucky.

One inch and we would have kissed. Jasper frowns at the thought. *Another inch and I could have crushed her.*

Fish pops up from nowhere and lands on Jasper's head, and both of them let out a howl as Jasper staggers to his feet in haste and turns poor Fish into a furry Frisbee.

"Great," I say, struggling to rise.

Jasper lends me a hand and we stand, dazed, assessing the wreckage. Picture frames are flat on their faces, the lamp is on its side, and the array of books on the coffee table have been scattered on the floor. And in the kitchen a bag of flour has been knocked to the ground, blanketing the floor like snow.

"I'm so sorry." Jasper growls over at Sherlock who's busy cowering in the corner. And Fish has somehow managed to lodge herself on top of the china cabinet that houses my teapot collection, a good seven feet off the ground.

"Don't apologize. It's clear he's missed her company." I shoot a look over to Sherlock who quickly buries his face under his paws.

Jasper groans at the wreckage. "Let me clean this up."

After fifteen minutes—of nonstop straightening, sweeping, and some light cursing, the two of us manage to not only butt heads on more than one occasion—quite literally, but we manage to return the cottage to its previous state despite the fact it played host to the animal wars. We stagger out of the kitchen just in time to find the furry little warriors each curled up on opposite ends of the sofa, fast asleep as if they weren't capable of such carnage to begin with.

A quiet laugh bounces through Jasper's chest. "Are you up for a cup of coffee?"

"If I didn't know better, I'd think you just read my mind."

Jasper and I drop Sherlock off back at home in the event the troublesome duo decides to reprise their kickboxing whirlwind. We head over to the Cottage Café and each pick up a latte to go and head out to the point to the left of the inn.

Waves crash over the boulders that press against the evergreens, the ocean is the color of slate steel, and the sky is hooded with dark angry clouds. The wind picks up just a notch, but I'm still plenty warm from my impromptu workout.

Jasper takes a breath, and I watch as his chest rises and falls.

Too quiet. She'll think I'm not interested. I don't want that. I want her to know that I'm most certainly interested. That I care about her thoughts—especially those related to the case.

My mouth falls open. "You wouldn't by chance be buttering me up with a walk along the beach in hopes I'll tell you all I know about the case, would you?" I can't help but giggle at the thought because I happen to know I'm right.

"I've been tougher on people."

A dull laugh pumps from me. "So where are *you* with the case?"

He pauses a moment to stare at the ocean. "How about we hold off on that for a moment? I've had the case on my mind all day. It's kind of nice to be one with nature."

"Be careful what you say. We've been one with the ocean before. Come to think of it, those two we left behind were responsible for that natural disaster as well."

"We should ditch them more often," he teases and I bubble with laughter.

"We should."

Nice laugh. His gaze rakes over my features, hot as coal. *Nice everything. Her temperament toward me, typically not so nice. But who knows? We might be making headway.*

A secretive smile plays on my lips, but I won't give it.

"Since you were kind enough to bring me flowers"—I say, ticking my head toward the woods—"I'll show you my secret hideaway." I navigate us to a dirt trail that leads up the rocky crag. My foot nearly slips and Jasper offers me his hand. I can't help but stare at it an inordinate amount of time.

"I promise I don't bite." His lips twitch again like maybe he does.

I can't help but glance skyward at that one. "Then you have no idea how much you're disappointing my family and friends." I take his hand and he helps me along for the next few feet of the trail.

"Just your family?" He sharpens those devilish eyes over mine.

"Why do I sense the fact you've bitten more than your fair share of women?"

He groans, "I would say you have very astute senses. But in my defense, I thought I had finally settled down."

"So does that mean you're ready to ramp up your playboy ways again?"

"Not in the least." He grimaces. "I've always been a one-woman man."

My brows bounce with approval as I lead us just past a thicket of sweetgums with their leaves in a spectacular shade of crimson and point to my treasure. A stone bench sits perched near the edge of the cliff, and its very surface is decorated with blue and jade sea glass in a mosaic pattern that mimics the motion of the ocean. "Georgie made it for me. I have no idea how she managed to haul it out in the middle of nowhere, but to quote her, she has her ways."

"Georgie is clearly a genius."

"That she is. And she's just as much a hazard. We went to see Jeannie Branch, and Georgie bought out most of her inventory and had it sent to my sister's shop. Suffice it to say, Macy was not amused. I think a lawsuit might be pending. Know of any good lawyers?"

"My brother, but I wouldn't put you in his hands." *And believe me, he would love to have you in his hands.* His brows bounce with the thought.

A laugh bubbles from me. "I guess we have that in common. My brother specializes in family practice. And is it terrible of me to say that Macy has already requested a meeting with any male siblings you might have?"

Now it's him enjoying a quick burst of laughter.

We take a seat, and suddenly it's painfully clear exactly how short this bench really is. Wow, he's going to think my goal was to end up in his lap. It wouldn't be the worst thing, but it wouldn't be the best, considering he's decided I shouldn't speak to anyone else regarding poor Kaitlynn's murder. But I'm pretty sure if you find the body, it gives you license to pry all you want.

Jasper sucks in a quick breath. "All of my brothers are single—and for good reason."

"So they're a lot like you?" I couldn't help it. He walked into that one.

His brows pinch in the middle. "They're a lot like you. They don't play well with others." *I couldn't help it. She walked into that one.*

"I'm not laughing," I say right through a silly grin, half afraid he might be prying into my mind. I look right at him and hook my gaze to his.

I bet you've never caught a killer in your life, I say as clear as I can in an effort to jar him.

He tips his head to the side, his brows pinching in the middle.

Not an unreasonable reaction to my intense staring, but any detective worth the salt of his badge would have piped up in order to dampen the blow to his ego.

I think.

"Bizzy"—he's inspecting me at close range, sweeping those high beams of his over my face, and I can feel each heated inch—"without overthinking it, what's your favorite food?"

"Kettle corn." I wince as I realize what I said.

"Kettle corn?"

"No judging. You said without overthinking it. Had you asked me to think it through, I would have said lobster in butter sauce."

"The kettle corn is far more budget friendly."

"Okay, my turn," I say, butting my shoulder to his playfully. "Without overthinking it, what's your favorite way to spend your free time?"

"Just like this."

"Really?"

"Yes. I love nature. I love relaxing. My dad used to say I would be the first to retire in the family." His chest bounces with a quiet laugh. "And believe me, I'm hoping

ADDISON MOORE & BELLAMY BLOOM

he's right. But I also love my work. I've made a career out of catching the bad guys. There's something very fulfilling in that." He tucks his head in close, his eyes never leaving mine. "And I can understand why you want to help with the case."

Those hypnotic eyes—the hypnotic, intoxicating scent of his spiced cologne. I'm not sure how much more of him I can handle—at least not in this close proximity. Restraining myself is asking far too much from my hormones.

I clear my throat as I come to. "Ah, so we finally made it to the case. We've come full circle. I suppose you want to know what Cameron Weiss had to say."

"I know he probably deflected. Who did he implicate?"

"Chris Davidson." I shrug because he's right. "Cameron said Kaitlynn and Chris were on the rocks. That the day before the murder she stopped by Cameron's place and told him she was breaking it off with Chris. Cameron is sure it's Chris who killed her, but he said he didn't tell you because he's afraid of retribution from the Davidson family. He said he has full faith that you would piece it together."

Jasper's gray eyes shoot a quick glance to the sea. "You're right. He didn't tell me. I'll make a note of it." He nods. "Look, Bizzy, I get it. Narrowing down suspects can be satisfying. The adrenaline rush can be addictive. And"—a breath expires from him—"it can be dangerous. So far, I think you've experienced the first two. Bizzy, I don't want you to get to three. I'm armed. I'm guessing you're not."

"I have a can of mace on my keychain, thank you very much."

"I can kill someone who is trying to kill me. At best you can momentarily blind them. And if they come after you with a gun or a knife like they did Kaitlynn"—he shakes his head as if he were searching for words—"I don't want to think what could happen to you."

"I think you just painted a picture. I guess I hadn't thought about it."

"Think about it. You're a smart woman. You run the inn like a well-oiled machine. You have everything going for you. I'd hate to see you put yourself in danger for no reason."

"No reason? Are you calling Kaitlynn no reason?"

"I don't mean to sound callous when I say this, but she's not coming back. You're still here. Believe me when I say mingling with potential suspects greatly decreases your odds of remaining on the right side of the soil. Bizzy, I want you to surrender the desire to seek out more suspects." His cheek flinches. "I'm not supposed to do this, but since you were friends with the deceased, and since you've already charged in headfirst into this investigation, I'll keep you updated. If you want, you can throw out theories, tell me anything you know, all of your thoughts. I'll allow you to remain on the fringe. I won't hide things from you." He bears into me with his heavy gaze. "I promise."

A wave crests the top of the embankment and the sea spray baptizes us with its salty brine.

"We should get back," I say and we start down the dirt trail as the daylight quickly dims. We make our way up the beach, and soon enough we're back to the rows of cottages behind the inn. I've always appreciated the walk, but with the thick silence swimming between us, it feels far too long.

Jasper walks me to my door and pauses. His lips twist in a knot.

What am I going to do with her?

There's a softness to him that I haven't seen before, and each time his eyes connect with mine, a bite of heat explodes in my stomach.

"I'd invite you in, but Fish seems to think your hair doubles as catnip." It's both thick and glossy, and my fingers have been trembling to run through it ever since he landed horizontal over me hours ago.

"She's not the only girl who thinks that." ***Wrong move. She's going to think I'm all ego and a fervent womanizer. I might have been at one point, but that's not who I am anymore.***

"I'm positive she's not." I lift my fingers to his hair and quickly slick it back the way I've been craving all night.

Jasper leans in and caresses my cheek with his thumb, one quick heated stroke, but I can still feel him there like a line of fire.

I wonder what she'd do if I kissed her? Probably test out the mace.

A tiny laugh brews in my chest, and his eyes widen with wonder as to what I'm finding so funny.

A laugh. Is that a good sign? Does she want a kiss? Or maybe she thinks I'm a joke. One thing is for sure. I cannot read this one.

"I think you're pretty easy to read." I shrug and his eyes widen just a notch. Okay, so maybe I shouldn't do that with Jasper. It's fun to tug with other people's sanity, but I think I'm trying his enough already. "Um"—I clear my throat—"I bought your coffee and showed you my secret hideout." I bat my lashes up at him, hoping he'll take the hint. Heaven knows I've never asked for a kiss in my life, and I'm not about to start now.

"You comped my coffee." His lips twitch at the tips, but he's too stubborn to smile. "And you showed me Georgie's beautiful artwork."

"Boy—you really are difficult, you know that?"

"Only on days that end in Y."

And not surprisingly, my blood begins to boil.

"Well then, I hope you enjoyed your coffee and your official tour of the grounds, Detective Wilder."

She's back to formal monikers. I've ticked her off good. He frowns at the discovery, as he should.

"Bizzy"—he leans in impossibly close—"I think I'm going to kiss you goodnight."

"Do you always announce your next move?"

"Only when I'm checking for clearance."

"If the runway gets any clearer, this traffic controller just might fall asleep," I tease.

He winces. "Then I'd better not bore you."

Jasper leans in and my eyes close as a mild jolt jumps from his mouth to mine, and he lingers over me in this sweet way.

He pulls back, and I catch the rise and fall of his Adam's apple.

"Goodnight, Bizzy. Thank you for the coffee and the tour. I thoroughly enjoyed both."

I nod, still blissfully dazed from having his mouth over mine.

It happened. That vampire that's been stalking me— oh heck, that I've been thinking about nonstop, effortlessly just walked us over to first base. And I'll be the last to complain.

A small, cynical part of me wonders if that was all a ploy to keep me off his case. If it was, his brilliance far outshines the sun.

I head inside with a goofy grin plastered to my face.

Jasper Wilder just kissed me senseless, and yet I still very much plan on tracking down my next suspect.

He was right. It's addictive. And now I can add Jasper's kisses to my growing list of addictions.

But nothing he said tonight is about to detour me from doing what I have to.

Sammy Walton, I'm coming for you.

13

"A chaste kiss?" Macy looks as if the thought alone has the power to make her sick.

"What does that even mean?"

"It means it was polite," I say, snuggling into my sweater at the memory. "It was nice."

"Bleh." Macy pretends to gag. "Let's hope his next move is a lot less polite and far more naughty."

It's the morning after, and both Macy and Georgie yanked a confession out of me as to how my *date* with Jasper ended last night. Just to be clear—I called it a business meeting and they referred to it as a date.

The three of us stand at the counter of the Cottage Café, and the morning rush just cleared up long enough for me to take a breather.

My gaze shifts outside where I can see from the window that the ocean is restless, dark and stormy, the whitewash slapping against the shore ever so violently. A few tourists enjoy a stroll in the sand, and the cobbled path just above that has a smattering of dog walkers.

Fish sits curled up in a ball on the brick perch that divides the café from the grassy strip to the left just before you get to the woods. God bless, Fish. That creature can sleep through anything.

"So where did you go?" Macy scoffs as she struggles to hook my attention with the wave of her hand. Her blonde hair is pulled back into a whippet of a ponytail and she's dressed in a long cable knit sweater, the color of burnt red autumn leaves. "You said Sherlock and Fish destroyed your place and then what?"

"You know what." Georgie smacks her on the arm. A silly grin rides on her face as if she *knows*—and what she knows looks pretty salacious. Her gray hair is styled and curled around her shoulders and she's wearing her work clothes, which for Georgie consists of heavily stained and paint-splattered overalls. "You were doing it on the sofa, weren't you? You never made it to the bedroom." She wags her finger at me. "You are a wily girl, Bizzy Baker. I have always suspected this about you."

"Georgie." I close my eyes. "Yes, we were doing it. We were *walking*." I take a moment to blink a quick smile at the two of them. "I took him to my secret place out at the edge of the embankment." I look to Georgie. "To that bench you gave me a few years back."

Macy's mouth falls open. "To the bench she gave you in hopes you'd be swept to sea?"

A deep groan works its way up my throat. "Macy— Georgie would never want me to be swept out to sea."

Georgie hitches her head to the side. "I might want that—a little bit, sometimes."

"All right, you clowns. That was all that happened. You can resume as normal once again. What's going on with your lives, anyway?"

Macy grunts, "I've got a wall of inventory I need to miraculously make disappear. And you know what? Shockingly, the stuff is selling like organic hot cakes. I mean, at first I was blowing it out just so I could make my way around the shop but, yesterday, I hiked the prices up and it's still selling like organic hot cakes."

Georgie moans with a smile, her shoulders rising to her ears. "Mmm, hot cakes. I'll take that for breakfast. Throw in one of those apple cinnamon walnut thingies. I'm feeling fearless today. I have a lot of work to do if I plan on having an entire table to myself at the Harvest by the Cove Festival."

Macy makes a face. "That goes double for me. Who thought this shindig was a good idea again?"

"Mayor Woods," I say her name low in the event it works as an incantation and I accidentally conjure up the witch.

"Mack?" Macy rolls her eyes. "Please don't give her the honor of calling her Mayor Woods. The girl is despicable. We're supposed to hate her, remember?"

Georgie sucks in a quick breath. "Why are we supposed to hate her? I can hate with the best of them, missy."

"We don't need to hate her," I'm quick to correct, lest the hating commence Georgie style and we end up with another body on our hands.

Macy shakes her head at Georgie. "Mack is a mean girl Bizzy went to school with. She stole every boy this girl showed an ounce of interest in and never has a nice thing to say about anyone. The only reason she got elected is because nepotism is alive and well."

"Not true," I say. "She got elected because when her father retired, people had a familiarity about her. Think about it. Her father and her grandfather were mayor before her. I can't think of a time Cider Cove didn't have a Mayor Woods at the helm."

Macy tosses up a hand. "Maybe so, but this one is going to sink the ship."

"Oh." Georgie shoves an elbow into my sister's ribs. "Cider Cove is unsinkable. Just like the *Titanic*." She gives a little wink. "Now get those hot cakes a cookin', young lady. Those hot cakes give me inspiration like nothing else, and I've got a million bottles to break before *I* get cooking on those mosaics. Keep an eye out when you're walking by the trash. You just wouldn't believe the treasures some people throw away." She heads off toward a table near the window.

Macy glances back. "I always think of you when I see trash, Georgie!" she calls out, and Georgie tosses a hand up at her. Macy and Georgie love to dish it out to one another, but it's all in fun. I think.

Macy leans in. Her glowing blue eyes are highlighted by perhaps a smidge too much mascara, but Macy is beautiful any way you slice her.

"All right, the gray witch is gone." Her lips turn at the tips. "You did it on the couch, didn't you?"

I avert my eyes. "I'm not going to bother with an answer."

"Okay, so how's the case going, Detective Baker?"

"It's going."

I quickly put in an order of hot cakes for Georgie before grabbing a cinnamon roll out of the bakery shelf.

Macy pulls my ooey gooey apple walnut wonder to herself, so I pluck another one out for Georgie.

"It's hard," I say. "I mean, there's a lot of finger-pointing, most of which is in the fiancé's direction. But there's still one woman I met at the beach that night I'm hoping to speak with. A woman by the name of Sammy Walton. I have no clue how to find her. And believe me, I've tried my hand at cyberstalking. Any ideas of how to track her down?"

"Sammy Walton?" She shakes her head while fiddling with her phone. "It says here she and Kaitlynn were sorority sisters." She shoves the phone my way, and there's a picture of the two of them in front of a white colonial mansion.

"How did you find that?" I take the phone from her to better examine it.

"I looked up their names together, and that's the first thing that popped up."

"Yeah, but where is she today? Sammy might be the missing piece to the puzzle."

"She's probably local. Hey? I bet she told Jasper where he can find her. He's the homicide detective, right? So, just ask your boyfriend." She gives a smug grin.

"Funny." I think on it a moment. "I can't ask Jasper because it might tip him off that I'm still investigating, but maybe I can ask Jeannie? I'll just head over and let her know I sold out of most of the Natural Beauty products. I bet she'll have the answer for me."

"Text her right now."

I pull out my phone and do just that, and she quickly lets me know she's out of supplies but will let me know when I can get more.

"Dead end." I flash my phone at my sister.

Jasper strides in with Sherlock Bones by his side, and Macy feigns a sigh.

"Enter Prince Charming." She gives me a firm shove in his direction. "Just ask, Bizzy."

"No," I hiss as he comes in close.

Jasper nods our way. His hair is still damp from the shower. The prickly stubble on his cheeks highlights those searing gray eyes, and my stomach explodes with heat just being near him like this—especially after that kiss.

"Macy, Bizzy"—his lips stretch into an all too brief smile when he nods my way—"good morning, ladies."

Macy hitches her thumb at me. "Bizzy wants to investigate a woman by the name of—Sammy Wilson?" She squints my way, and I close my eyes and groan. "Anyway, she's hit a dead end. Maybe you can help her with that." She snatches the cinnamon roll from the counter and slinks off before I can poison her food.

Jasper sheds a wide grin as those shining eyes of his pierce through mine. "Sammy *Walton*," he kindly corrects.

"I knew that." I shrug up at him.

He purses his lips a moment. ***And I wonder what else she knows.***

He flexes a short-lived smile my way. "Are you busy later this afternoon?"

"I'm always busy. That's my name, remember?" A flirtatious smile graces my lips as Sherlock bounces up on his hind legs.

Good one, Bizzy! Sherlock bounds from side to side. *Treat, please! Treat! Treat!*

Jasper pulls at Sherlock's leash until he sits at attention. "If you're free, I'm heading over to see her. I'll gladly give you a lift."

A lift to see Sammy Walton?

"Yes, I'm free." I blink at him, wide-eyed. "Why the sudden reversal? Don't tell me my lips are that powerful because that would just be cheesy."

And quite possibly true. He sighs and I can't help but smile. *Great. Now she thinks I'm gunning for second base.* He glances to my lips. *Although, I wouldn't mind checking out first again.*

"It's not a reversal," he insists. "We'll be in a very public setting. No interrogating on your part. Deal?"

"Deal." I may or may not be telling the truth, but that's not the point.

I take his order, add in a piece of bacon for Sherlock, and deliver Georgie the hot cakes set to inspire her already wild imagination.

"Hey?" She pulls me back by the sleeve. "Did you score date number two?"

ADDISON MOORE & BELLAMY BLOOM

I glance to Jasper as he heads to the beach with Sherlock, scone and coffee in hand.

"I did," I whisper it low like a secret, and she claps her hands and hoots.

"I knew it! Don't you worry, Bizzy. He'll land you horizontal on the sofa before you know it."

My stomach cinches with heat at the thought. That's exactly what I'm afraid of.

He's hand-feeding me Sammy Walton.

But why?

14

At exactly four o'clock, Detective Jasper Wilder picks me up looking rather, well, very un-detective like. He's donned jeans and a flannel with red and black checkers, and it only seems to make his eyes shine like sirens all the more.

We make small talk as he drives us up the road to the orchard that butts up against the Cottage Inn's property line. The acreage of orchards spans out seemingly to the four corners of the earth, and there's an oversized barn just beyond the parking lot with a general store and the weigh and pay station for the apple pickers.

I sigh, filled with nostalgia as we come upon the large wooden sign.

"Cider Cove Orchards," I say. "I must have visited this place almost every fall when I was growing up. I was friends with Valerie Montgomery. Her parents own this place."

"I've been up a few times myself. My parents took my siblings and me."

"Ooh, siblings. I think I've already warned you. Macy has called dibs on your brothers. So how soon can they audition for her official plus one?"

He belts out a short-lived laugh as we park and quickly hop out.

The air is crisp and scented with cinnamon cider as we head on over to what looks to be a fairground. There are bounce houses for the kids, face painting, press your own cider, game booths with prizes, wagon rides, and a man dressed as a giant caramel apple taking pictures with a group of teenagers.

"Please, tell me about the siblings," I say as I butt my shoulder to his. "Macy will smother me in the night if I don't get the lowdown."

"In that case I'd better cough up all I know. I do like to keep you safe, Bizzy." His eyes meet with mine and there's a softness to them that lets me know he means it. And the slight reference to me staying out of the case isn't lost on me either. "I've got three brothers and a sister. I fall dead in the middle."

My mouth opens with a smile. "Wow. Well, don't stop there. I want to know all about them."

"That's easy. They're all local. My sister Ella is married and has a baby on the way next spring. She works as a clerk for the fishing company her husband owns. That's how they met. My brother Max—Maximus, owns a restaurant named after himself called *Maximus*. Don't let the small ego fool you. He's pretty full of himself." His chest bounces with a laugh. "He's a good guy, though. My brother Jamison is the attorney, family law, so our brothers have that in common."

"Ooh, they do. And don't forget they will always come in handy when there's a divorce on the horizon."

He cinches a short-lived smile my way, and my insides burn with heat.

"I'd stay away from Vegas if I were you."

A laugh bubbles from me. "All right, go on. You have one brother to go."

"Dalton. He's the football coach for Ward University."

"No kidding? Is that why they're always losing?" I bump his shoulder one more time as he tips his head and laughs to the sky.

"Okay, you're funny. But if they keep up this non-winning streak—he's forbidden me from saying the L word—he won't have a job come winter."

"Ouch. In that case, go Ward. I hope my peers from Dexter can forgive me for that one."

"You should come to a game. In fact, Ward is playing Dexter in two weeks. I've got spare tickets."

"Really? I'd love to. But I could never get Emmie to come with me. I guess I could ask my brother."

"This is me asking you."

"What?" I inch back just as we approach the acres of apple trees all dotting the landscape in tight neat rows. "Jasper Wilder, are you up to no good?"

His brows swoop low. "I might be. But that's for me to know and you to find out."

"Someone was paying attention in middle school." I laugh as I pick up a basket and we head on into a section of the orchard marked *Pink Ladies*.

He cocks his head to the side. "So, is that a yes?"

A group of women about my age make their way past us carrying a basket filled with delicious pink globes, and each one of them gives Jasper the once-over as they crane their necks to get a better look at him.

I'm sure he gets that all the time. He's heart-stoppingly attractive. A handsome man like Jasper is practically a roadside hazard in any situation that calls for women to pay attention to where they're going. I'm not sure why he's paying attention to me.

His brows depress again. *She's going to say no. Shoot. I shouldn't have led with that. I should have saved it. Heck, maybe I should have asked her to dinner. Somewhere nice like Maximus.*

"Yes. To the game." I offer a warm yet brief smile. "But I'll be wearing my Dexter sweatshirt."

A dull laugh rumbles through his chest. "I wouldn't want it any other way."

"Good." I point to a tree dripping with blush-colored ornaments that look as juicy as they do sweet. "So, three single brothers?"

"All single." He makes a face. "You sound like you're interested."

And I hope that's not the case. He openly frowns.

"Definitely not the case. Just surprised," I say, plucking at the highest apple I can reach and chucking it into the basket. "I mean, I'm assuming they all look like you. That just seems odd they're single."

He chuckles a moment. "They're odd and that about explains their inability to land a lady. But I'm one to talk."

"Oh right." I wince. "The counselor who's dating the deputy now. You mentioned you dated for four years? That's longer than some people stay married."

He tosses a lazy grin my way. "Yeah, you."

"All right. You leave my Vegas wedding alone. At least I got to check it off my bucket list."

He shakes his head. "That doesn't count. If marriage is something you want out of life, you need to go for the gold. Everyone deserves their shot at happiness." He tosses an apple into the bucket. "Or misery, depending on your views."

My mouth falls open. "You think marriage is a miserable institution?"

"Not me. My parents might think so. They've been divorced for years now."

"Join the broken family club. I hated it when my parents divorced. I would much rather have gone through anything but that."

"I agree." He tosses in a few more apples. "And that's exactly why I'm going to be in it for keeps." He closes his eyes a moment. "I hope."

"Me, too. I'll do everything I can to be sure that the person I'm getting involved with is the one for me. I want it all, the long golden marriage, lots of kids, the white picket fence, dogs, cats, maybe even something reptilian to keep things interesting."

His chest bounces with the thought. "Dalton brought home a snake once. My mother did not feel that made things interesting. She made him get rid of it and told him he could have all the snakes he wanted once he was on his own."

"And that begs the question. How many snakes does he have?"

"Zero. He's too tied to that university to have anything that needs to depend on him."

"Well, then he's wise. It's hard to own a pet and then not be able to spend time with them. I see it happen all the time. The Country Cottage Inn is always booked in part because we're the only place that allows animals. But even some of those would be cooped up all day if we didn't offer daycare services."

"I didn't know the inn offered daycare services."

"Yup. It's open to all of Cider Cove. I run it with ample staff. We have an indoor and outdoor facility just off the back of the inn. You should come by some time and I'll show you."

"I will. I'll bring Sherlock. He'll get a kick out of it." His chest expands as he lands a few more apples into the cart. "So, you ready to talk about Kaitlynn Zimmerman?"

Any trace of a smile melts right off my face. "Smooth, detective. You dressed down, brought me to a feel-good place, and loosened my good senses just enough to see if I'd spill what I know."

He closes his eyes a moment. "You are good. But you're wrong. If I wanted to shake away your good senses it wouldn't be to get you to spill what you know."

My eyes widen a moment as a searing heat rips through me.

"I'm sorry." He holds up a hand. ***And yet I meant it.***

He looks as if he feels equally bad for his actions as he does his thoughts.

"Don't apologize. A man with an ego like yours can't help it."

Ego? There's that. She hates me. He pierces me with those brilliant gray eyes. *Good thing I have always been up for a challenge.*

"What about Kaitlynn? Did you get a break in the case?"

"Maybe." He's back to frowning. "You asked about her engagement ring."

"And you confirmed she was wearing it the day she died."

"What made you ask?"

"The ring in her purse. That was no ordinary hunk of diamonds. It just looked like an engagement ring to me."

"Me, too." He looks pensively into the rows of trees before us.

"Did you contact her mother? I mean, maybe she knows something about it. Trust me. My mother would know if I happened to be in possession of two different engagement rings."

"Kaitlynn and her mother were estranged."

I wince hard. "That's right. I think Rissa mentioned it. I guess I won't pass Detective 101 for failing to memorize facts."

"Don't be so hard on yourself. Her father didn't have a clue as to who the ring belonged to, but we're assuming it's Kaitlynn's for now. Bizzy, can you think of anything else from the night of the murder that could move the case along?"

It's my turn to gaze out at the acres of apple trees that extend before us as I consider this.

"You know, after Rissa and Kaitlynn had their big argument, Kaitlynn told me that Rissa was mad because someone in their social circle was seeing Rissa's boyfriend. I guess it wasn't behind her back because Rissa seemed to know about it. But seeing how heated she was, I'm betting she just found out. Maybe it was Rissa's engagement ring? Maybe she took it off and it ended up in Kaitlynn's possession?"

"Sounds plausible. I'll have to talk to Rissa again. As in, I'll do it alone." His head ticks to the side as if to emphasize his point.

"Where's the fun in that? Besides, I'm a woman. She's much more likely to open up to me."

"I don't know about that." He gives a wistful shake of the head. "She seemed pretty willing to open up to me the day I interrogated her. In fact, she was willing to give me a whole lot more than I was asking for."

"Okay, I get it. She was into you and wanted to see how fast she could pin you to a mattress." Our eyes hook to one another for an uncomfortable amount of time, and I don't dare pry into his thoughts. "But I still think she wouldn't open up to you about her ex."

"Yes, but she might know the story behind the ring," he asserts.

"Or she could lie in an effort to garner that lovely piece of ice. Speaking of her ex—or her current cheating boyfriend, what about Ben?"

Jasper's chest expands with his next breath. "Ben O'Riley is on assignment for an advertising firm. He's a photographer who has been in Singapore for the last six weeks. I've spoken to him, and he's offered sufficient evidence that he's been there. He's due back in town soon. He seemed extremely devastated to hear Kaitlynn had passed away."

"Extremely?" The word echoes in my mind long after he's said it.

His phone rings, and he frowns down at the screen.

"Excuse me for a minute. It's the precinct. I've got to take it."

"Absolutely. Go ahead. I'll make sure we have more apples than we can afford."

Jasper takes off just as a loud group of teenagers head in this direction, and behind them is a brunette about my age, clad in overalls and the look of utter exhaustion written on her face. She's got on a pair of bright yellow leather gloves that look far too big for her hands as she brushes the loose hair from her eyes with her arm. Her dark hair is pulled into a ponytail, and there's something vaguely familiar about her.

She steps in close, and I see the apple-shaped nametag pinned to her shirt that reads *Sammy* in bright green letters.

"Sammy?" I ask, quickly glancing back to make sure Jasper isn't about to pop out from the trees and bust me for making a move on his investigation.

"That's me." She's suddenly bright-eyed and bushy-tailed as she makes her way over. "How can I help you? You need a picker?" She grabs a tall stick lying on the ground and hands it my way. "If you ask me, the sweetest apples are up near the top. We've got ladders sprinkled around if you're feeling brave. But be careful. Unless you're here with a pair of strong arms to catch you in the event you fall, I wouldn't do it."

A brief vision of falling into Jasper's beefy arms runs through my mind, and a rush of adrenaline runs through me at the thought.

"I'm no damsel in distress, but I'll heed your warning and stay away. Hey, I think I met you. The night of the bonfire?"

"Oh." She closes her eyes. "That's right. You had the cute dog. I just hate thinking about that night. I was friends with the girl who was killed. Can you believe that? Someone really had it out for her." Sammy looks to the ground as if lost in grief.

And if I'm not mistaken, it was Sammy who was talking about Kaitlynn in past tense that evening before she supposedly knew the poor girl was gone.

"I can't imagine how things could have gone that wrong," I say. "I guess they think it was a crime of passion. I mean, that kind of thing almost always points to the boyfriend, right?"

Her chest thumps at the thought. "Not this time. Chris wouldn't hurt a fly. Okay, so maybe he'd hurt a fly, but he wouldn't stab his girlfriend to death. And to do something like that in public? You'd have to be insane."

Wow, he is insane, but aren't we all?

"Yes," I say hypnotically. "I mean, I firmly believe whoever did this was insane—at least in the moment." I add the qualifier in the event she needs the out. "So, if Chris didn't do it, who did? She didn't have a secret man on the side, did she?"

"Kaitlynn?" She leans back as if the thought were incomprehensible. "I don't know. I don't think so. If she did, she was hiding the fact really well. But Chris didn't hide it." Her lips pull back. "He had someone else on the side."

"What?" I squawk so loud the teenagers down the way turn around momentarily. "How could he have someone else? I heard they were engaged?" And on the rocks, but I'm not giving up that little tidbit.

A small laugh bucks through her. "There are no hard and fast rules to being a turkey. And Chris has always been ripe for the Thanksgiving table, if you know what I mean. There were whispers in our circle that he was stepping out on her. I figured it would get to her eventually."

"Oh. Well, I manage the inn where she worked as a waitress, and I happened to see her arguing with her stepsister Rissa that night. Maybe it was Rissa who was sneaking off with Chris?"

She grimaces at the thought. "Heavens no. Rissa has her own problems. She didn't need any of Kaitlynn's trouble."

"That's right," I say, hoping I can lead her down a thorny path. "Kaitlynn mentioned that Rissa was angry because someone was trying to steal *her* boyfriend. I guess I had it confused."

"Don't worry. It is confusing. And yes, Rissa was ticked because Kaitlynn's best friend was putting the moves on her boyfriend. As far as I know, Rissa dumped him."

"Kaitlynn's best friend? Jeannie Branch?"

Her mouth falls open as she chokes on a laugh. "I can't believe you know all my friends. You must have been really close to Kaitlynn at work." *Dear Lord. What else does she know? Exactly how much would Kaitlynn have told this woman?*

"We were," I lie. "So, who was the girl who was after Chris?"

"After? *Pfft*. You mean *with*. Chris didn't hold back with that one."

I'm not letting the cat out of the bag. I've already said way too much. Hannah would kill me if she knew I was talking about her to a perfect stranger no less.

"Oh, wait. Kaitlynn told me her name." I snap my fingers. "It's coming to me. It was Anna—or something like that."

"Hannah." She nods, wide-eyed as if marveling at the fact I had it on the tip of my tongue. *How about that? I didn't have to tell her. It sounds like Kaitlynn was blabbing all her secrets at work. Kaitlynn never did know when enough was enough.* Her features grow dark as she assesses me.

"Hannah! Yes!" I slap my knee. "Oh, Kaitlynn hated her."

"Of course, she hated her. She's always hated Hannah. There was always this unspoken competition going on between them. Personally, I think Hannah was trying to swipe Kaitlynn's fiancé just to prove that she could. Some girls are just catty that way to each other."

So Chris was cheating on Kaitlynn with some girl named Hannah. I bet that's exactly why they were on the rocks.

"I have a Hannah in my life, and believe me I don't care for her. And yes, she's made it a habit to swipe any and every man out of my paws." I'm looking at you, Mackenzie Woods. Jasper flits through my mind, and my stomach cinches at the thought of her swiping him and those delicious kisses away.

Sammy's brows jump as if she were amused. "You know what they say. If you lose them, they were never really yours to begin with."

I try to shrug it off, but the words sting nonetheless "So, what's Hannah doing these days? I bet she's whistling Dixie because she gets Chris all to herself now." I had to go with it.

"You'd be wrong. They're staying far away from one another. Rumor has it, he cut her off after the murder. I guess an eternal absence makes the heart grow fonder, too. He's doing the right thing, though. He's finally showing Kaitlynn a little respect."

I shrug. "I guess a dead fiancée is enough to douse just about any philandering flame." Unless the philanderer is also the killer. "Where does Hannah work?"

Her eyes narrow in on mine. *Why all the questions?*

Jasper pops up out of nowhere, and I take a quick breath at the sight of him.

"It's you!" She points a gloved finger at him. "Are you two trying to set me up or something? Did you send your nosey girlfriend here to spy on me?"

Jasper takes a slow breath. *I leave her alone for five minutes and now this.*

"No!" I shake my head at her. "I promise, it's nothing like that. I really do work at the Country Cottage Inn. And I'm not his girlfriend. In fact, I'm nothing to him. I don't even *like* him."

Jasper shoots me a look. *Gee, thanks.*

My eyes widen his way as I silently ask him to go with it.

Sammy sighs hard as she examines the two of us. "Look, I don't know who killed Kaitlynn, but you're right." She gives me the stink eye. "This is probably a crime of passion. One thing is for sure. It was no accident. Especially not since Kaitlynn predicted her death."

Jasper leans in. "Are you saying Kaitlynn knew someone was angry enough to kill her?"

She shrugs. "It's something people say all the time, isn't it? If something happens to me, you'll know why."

My heart thumps wildly as if the answer to who killed Kaitlynn was about to bubble right out of her.

"So, who did she say she needed to watch out for?" I ask with bated breath.

"She was ambiguous about it. But she knew something bad was coming. She wanted to put it out there that she didn't feel safe." Someone calls her name from the oversized barn in the distance. "I gotta go. Try to solve this case, would you?" She glares at Jasper. "Kaitlynn deserves some justice." Her chest rises with her next breath as she looks to the two of us.

Maybe I told them the truth. Maybe I didn't. Maybe I'm not sure about it either.

She takes off, and I shudder in her wake.

"So?" Jasper stares me down with those white-hot spotlights he calls eyes. "What did you learn?"

My lips twist in protest, but in my heart I realize that withholding anything from him at this point would be petty. A woman was killed. This isn't a game.

"I'm not sure if she was telling the truth, but she said Rissa and Kaitlynn were arguing that night because Kaitlynn's best friend, Jeannie Branch, was trying to steal Rissa's boyfriend." I watch as his jaw becomes defined. "And that a girl named Hannah, who had a habit of irritating Kaitlynn, was trying to steal Chris. Heck, he was openly with her. Apparently, everyone in their circle knew about it."

"That had to have been hard." *I should know. I've been there.*

A breath catches in my throat.

"I'm sorry," I say and he takes a partial step back. "I mean, I thought maybe you might be able to commiserate a little."

"I can." He takes a breath. "A lot. That deputy my ex was involved with happened to be my best friend."

My gut cinches for him. "That's so terrible. I'm sorry, Jasper. I can't imagine how painful that must have been for you."

"I'm over it. Being in Cider Cove is exactly what I needed." He tilts his head, his eyes probing into mine. *This is exactly what I needed.*

I clear my throat. "Who's next on your list, detective?" I run my tongue absentmindedly over my lips, and his gaze falls to my mouth. His lids hang low, and his breathing grows shallow.

"Who's on your list, Bizzy?"

"Hannah, whoever she is."

"Hannah Osmond," he says it slow and low as if I had hypnotized the answer right out of him.

Did I just say that? His chest pumps. *I have got to watch my mouth around this woman. She'd be liable to get the nuclear codes from me if I had them.*

Nuclear codes? He has no clue he could do the same with me.

He takes a step in, and my feet duplicate the action until we're a breath away.

His fingers hitch a loose strand of hair behind my ear.

"Do you know what I've always wanted to do in an orchard?"

My lips part, but not a word comes out.

He nods just once. "Taste something sweet."

Jasper bows in and lands a soft kiss to my lips. *Yes, indeed, she does taste sweet.*

His mouth moves over mine as he kisses me senseless right here in the open for all to see as if he wasn't simply laying claim to my mouth, but he was laying claim to me.

My stomach detonates in a fireball as Jasper pulls me in close, his kisses growing more intense by the moment. I try my best to pry into his mind, but he's too far gone. It's nothing but a jumble of white noise. But I can feel the emotion behind his every move as he roams in my mouth, and it's unlike anything I've ever felt before.

Our kisses grow with ferocious intensity. I don't know what's happening between Jasper and me.

Could he really be using me to advance his case?

Or could this unimaginably handsome man truly be interested in a simple innkeeper like me?

Mackenzie Woods flits through my mind. As soon as she picks up on the fact that I'm falling for the good detective, she'll do her best to sink her claws into him. My heart breaks just thinking about it. Mackenzie is an inevitable pitfall we'll have to cross if things ever get serious.

Kaitlynn had a friend like Mackenzie, too—and I use the term *friend* loosely. I can already tell that Hannah Osmond isn't the kind of person I'd call a friend. But that won't stop me from pretending to be one in an effort to advance my own investigation.

I don't know what Jasper's intentions are, but one thing I know for sure. You can't fake a heated kiss like this.

Can you?

15

It's a quiet afternoon at the Cottage Café. Emmie has just come in for the day, looking bleary-eyed and groggy.

Just past the patio the ocean surges in heaving, intense gestures as the waves wallop over the sand with incomprehensible heft. The skies are thick with purple clouds, and the winds are picking up. All of Cider Cove has their fingers crossed that this storm will blow over in time for the Harvest at the Cove Festival coming up this weekend.

Emmie pins me in against the bakery shelf I just filled with my apple walnut cinnamon rolls.

"You're not going anywhere, Baker, until you spill every word of what happened at that orchard yesterday. And don't tell me it was innocent, because judging by that goofy grin you can't shake, I can tell it was anything but that."

"Don't you dare start without us," an all too familiar female voice chimes from behind, and I turn to find Macy and Georgie speeding this way. The matching gleam in their eyes lets me know they're equally hungry for gossip.

I can't help but make a face at my sister. Her hair is slicked straight and glossy as if she just had it blown out, and she's wearing a tight red dress that I let her borrow about six months ago and haven't seen since—until now.

Georgie is clad in navy, a newer kaftan that has orange stitching running up and down the front in the shape of tiny arrows. Her gray curls are piled high on top of her head, and she has a wooden beaded necklace on that she happens to wear each fall. If anything, Georgie's fashion sense is dictated by the seasons, which is something I totally appreciate about her. I'm sort of addicted to the seasons and the magic they bring myself.

"Okay, fine." I pick up a dishrag and begin wiping down the counter just as Emmie takes it away from me. "We kissed again." I shrug it off as if it were nothing.

Georgie gasps, "This is getting serious. The way he was strutting around town, snacking on your lips, you'd think the two of you were together."

"We're not together. With the exception, of course, when the two of us are in the exact same location. But other than that, we're both very much free agents."

Macy groans, "No, no, no. I'm the one that's supposed to have the exciting love life. You're sane and responsible. You're supposed to have been engaged to an accountant who owns an entire dresser full of argyle sweaters by now."

"But she's not." Emmie is quick to wag a finger at my sister. "She's busy kissing a homicide detective from Seaview—who, for the record, she's not dating."

Georgie waves off the idea. "They're dating. They just don't know it yet. It's a classic as far as romance stories go. They'll be married by next fall. Mark my words."

I gasp at the thought. Georgie is rarely wrong about these things.

"Take that back. I am not marrying that man. He's far too controlling for my taste."

Macy scoffs. "He's hot *and* he's controlling? My goodness, Bizzy, you just get everything, don't you?"

"Stop." I try my best to blink away the lunacy. "Look, I've got another suspect to question this afternoon."

Macy gags. "We don't care about your suspects. Back to the story. Once you left the orchard, did he try to take you to a second location?"

"Macy"—Emmie giggles—"you make it sound like a kidnapping."

My sister rolls her eyes. "It would have been if she was lucky. I can't believe my little sister gets to live out every single one of my fantasies."

"Your fantasies are depraved, by the way," I say.

"Please." Macy takes a moment to glare at the ceiling. "Do you want to know what I saw in the corner of my bathroom this morning?"

Emmie groans, "If this has to do with week old underwear, I think I can speak for all of us when I say we'll take a hard pass."

"No, not that." Macy looks crestfallen at whatever is about to pop from her mouth next—and with my sister you never know what that might be. "I saw two daddy long-leg spiders going at it."

Georgie leans in. "You mean they were fighting?"

"No." Macy bats her away. "They were getting busy. Do you know what that means?"

Emmie shakes her head. "That you need to work harder to keep your house clean?"

"No." Macy sighs. "That the spiders in my house are getting more action than I am."

"Ooh, speaking of which"—I suddenly brighten— "you'll love what I'm about to say next. Jasper has three brothers, and each of them is single."

The three of them gasp so loud the few customers we have all turn to gawk our way.

"We're fine." I'm quick to shoo everyone back to their own business. "Everything is just fine."

"It is now," Macy balks. "And when do I get to meet these single studly brothers?"

Emmie leans in as if she were suddenly interested in procuring one for herself. "Are they all homicide detectives?"

"No. There's Maximus, who owns a restaurant by the same name down in Seaview." The three of them swoon on cue. "There's Jamison, who practices family law like Huxley. And there's Dalton, who happens to be the head football coach for Ward University."

"Oh my goodness." Georgie clasps her heart as if she couldn't take it. "Each one sounds more delicious than the next. Please tell me he has a single father."

"He does, I think. In the least he's divorced."

Macy gets that wild look in her eyes that she gets when she is clearly scheming.

"Tell him we'll host a family reunion for his entire clan asap, right here at the inn."

"I can't tell him that. I'm not allowed to give away rooms for free."

Macy clicks her tongue. "Nobody said anything about free. You'll cover the cost."

A laugh bubbles from me. "Nice try. But I can't do that either. Anyway, I need to get going. I have to find out where I can speak to a girl named Hannah Osmond."

Macy twists her lips. "If I track her down, do you promise to introduce me to at least one of the Wilder brothers? The cutest of the bunch, please."

Emmie laughs. "I bet that would be Jasper, and he's already taken."

"You've got a deal, Macy." I'm quick to take her up on the offer. "Heck, if you could tell me where I can find Hannah, I'd introduce you to all three and his sister to boot."

Macy trots out of the café without bothering to say a word to any of us just as my phone bleats in the pocket of my apron and I fish it out.

It's a text from Jasper. I step away from Emmie and Georgie as they strike up a conversation about the harvest festival coming up.

Hey, Bizzy, just wanted to let you know I have a significant lead in the investigation. Promise me you won't look into things further. I'm closing in on the killer and don't want you putting yourself in harm's way.

My heartbeat ratchets up a few notches as I take in his words. Jasper must know who the killer is.

I quickly text back. **Thank you for the heads-up. I'll be sure to stay far away from your investigation.**

I hit send just as Macy trots my way with a spring in her step.

"Guess what, my sweet, albeit slightly nosey, little sister?" she trills as if she were about to burst with good news. "I know exactly where you can find a girl by the name of Hannah Osmond. In fact, I know where you can find her right now."

"Where?" It takes everything in me not to pull Macy in by her shirt.

"A place called The Rat Tat."

"The Rat Tat?" I ask as I snatch my purse from under the counter. "Emmie, I'm going to step out for a bit. I've got Nessa up front. If you need anything, give me a holler."

"Where are you going?" Emmie calls out as I make my way around the counter.

Georgie cackles and claps. "I bet that vampire told her to hurry down to Seaview because she's about to get lucky!"

"Wrong," I shout back as I look to my sister. "We're not headed to Seaview, are we?"

"Nope." She cinches her purse over her shoulder. "We're off to Edison!"

Both Georgie and Emmie groan because we all know nothing good happens in Edison.

With the exception of today.

Today, Kaitlynn Zimmerman's killer will be revealed to me in that seedy little town.

At least I'm hoping.

The Rat Tat is a skinny little building tucked between a cleaners and defunct flower shop. A large neon rat crawls high above the storefront with the words *The Rat Tat* glowing in an obnoxious hue of fluorescent green. The windows are decorated with all sorts of threatening artwork, and there's a smaller sign that boasts *fifteen percent off first tattoo! Inquire about our frequent buyer's program. Dirty thirty is free!*

Macy muses as we stare at the window together. "Do you think by dirty thirty they mean the birthday? Because I'm coming up on mine and I just might be feeling the need to commemorate it with a butterfly on my—"

"Okay, I don't want to know," I say, hauling her inside with me.

"What?" Her voice pitches to that faux innocent octave of hers. "I was just going to say my ankle."

"Not the ankle," a deep voice strums from behind the counter to our left, and we look over to find a tall beefy man, moderately handsome under all that guyliner and black lipstick. He's got a full-on Mohawk going and looks to be about our age. "The ankle is one of the more painful places to land a needle. I should know. I'm Rod, the owner."

"Ooh." Macy's eyes swirl like pinwheels at the punk rock cutie as she gravitates swiftly in his direction. I spot a girl behind the next counter, leafing through thick booklets as if she were on a mission, and I head over. She's far more demure looking than Rob by a punk rock mile. Her hair is the color of black coffee, and her eyes are a pretty shade of teal that I've never seen on a person before, and it makes me wonder if she's wearing contacts. Her nametag is secured to the lapel of her leather jacket, and I speed over in hopes to get a better look.

"Can I help you?" She glances briefly in my direction and her nametag flips, revealing the name *Hannah* written in large bold print.

Perfect.

"Oh yes," I say, trying to catch my breath. Who knew Macy could come through for me so quickly? She never did out her source. Regardless, I owe her three single Wilder brothers on a silver platter for this mystery-busting move. "I, uh, am looking to get a tattoo. My friend died recently, and I just…"

Words escape me for a moment. I'm not really going to get a tattoo, am I?

My goodness, it's as if this investigation has taken over my better senses. Not to mention the fact I came straight here after promising Jasper I'd stay out of it. But who could blame me? Macy went out of her way to procure this piece of investigative gold. And something tells me, Hannah, here, will be every ounce the precious metal—or better yet—the precious missing link to this murderous puzzle.

"I get it." Hannah shakes her head. "I just lost a friend, too."

Her eyes light up as if the thought thrilled her. And I can't help but frown. This is the girl that Sammy likened to Mack. Not that Sammy knew she was drawing the analogy—but, trust me, I got it loud and clear.

She pushes the oversized book in front of her my way. "How about something simple? There are tons of icons and symbols in this catalog that could serve as inspiration. Try to think of something that was meaningful to the both of you. That way, when you look at it, you'll think of them."

"That's a great idea. How about you? Are you getting a tattoo to commemorate your friend, too?" I pull the book my way and pretend to peruse the offerings.

"I don't think so." She just about scoffs when she says it. "I've got more than enough memories, thank you very much."

My eyes flit to hers. "It doesn't sound like the two of you got along very well."

"Oh, we got along plenty. My friend was actually murdered a few weeks back up in Cider Cove."

"Oh my goodness." I clasp my chest, but I don't have to feign distress. The thought still very much horrifies me. "I'm so sorry to hear that. And I can see why you'd think twice before commemorating her. That might be a very painful reminder."

"It would be—but for other, less obvious reasons." She shrugs. "Kaitlynn was ticked at me before she died, and now there's no way to go back and fix things. We were never that close to begin with. But I tried. Boy, I tried. Her friends weren't exactly all that nice to me. Once upon a time, they were my friends, too, but Kaitlynn had a way of squeezing all the good things I had out of my world and into hers."

Huh. That's almost the opposite of what Sammy said. But then, I suppose perspective is everything.

"I'm really sorry to hear it. Maybe she didn't realize what she was doing?"

A tiny laugh belts from her. "She knew. Kaitlynn always tried to make herself out to be the victim when it came to the two of us. That's how she got all our friends to turn against me. But, the truth is, I dated all those guys first. That crazy fiancé of hers? I dumped him a week before they became a thing."

Chris?

I shake my head in disbelief.

"Why would she turn the tables like that? It sounds almost maniacal, don't you think?"

"I don't have to think. I know. She did it because she could. Kaitlynn enjoyed being cruel to me. Back when we were kids, her mother and my father had an affair. She took it out on me. I didn't ruin her family, though. But that didn't stop her. I was the physical representation of her mother's sins. Every time she saw me, she practically smirked because she was relishing the fact she was exacting her revenge."

"So, how did she get her friends to believe you were having an affair with her boyfriend?" I catch myself and gasp.

What did she just say? She squints over at me as if probing my own mind for the answer. *There's no way she could possibly know that, unless—*

I shake my head abruptly. "I'm sorry. Not an affair. I meant, how did she convince them that you were trying to steal him? You said that was her go-to lie, right?"

"Oh, I see." She rolls her eyes to the ceiling. "Yeah, that was her MO. Just before she'd dump the turkey she was seeing, she'd spread rumors that I was sleeping with them. And sadly, all her friends believed her wild lies. But they weren't true." Her shoulders bounce.

"Was anyone sleeping with her fiancé? I mean, the last guy she was with before she died?"

"Yup. But it wasn't me. A mutual friend of ours said he was certain Kaitlynn learned the truth."

He? As in Cameron?

"So, who was her fiancé having an affair with? I mean, was it like a friend, a relative?" *Names*, I want to shout, *give me names*.

"It was a friend, a very close friend."

"Why would a very close friend do this to her? I wouldn't sleep with my friend's fiancé. You have to draw the line, right?"

"Not this ditz. She doesn't have a line or a moral compass. But she did have a vengeance she was looking to exact. A long time ago, when Kaitlynn's father finally got around to divorcing his cheating wife, he lost his mind and started embezzling large chunks of cash from the company he co-founded with two of his buddies. Let's just say his buddies weren't too thrilled when they found out. The government got involved and accused all three of them of trying to shortchange their clients, and they ended up doing time. Can you believe it? Two of them were innocent, and yet they had their lives turned upside down because of her ridiculous father. And, of course, once they were released, their lives were no better. They were officially felons, and no one in the business world would touch them with a ten-foot pole. It really screwed up their lives for good."

"Wow. So, what was the friend's name? The one whose father went to prison as an innocent man?" My heart slams over my chest again and again in anticipation of her answer. Whoever tried to steal Chris certainly had an axe to grind with Kaitlynn's father and Kaitlynn by proxy.

She shakes her head. "You wouldn't know her."

A group of older women enter the shop, giggling and reeking of vodka.

Hannah groans at the sight. "Having a location across the street from two different bars is both a blessing and a curse. I'd better help these women. Take your time."

She takes off and I do the same, snatching Macy by the elbow as we head for the door.

"Wait a minute!" Macy latches her hand over the doorframe before I suction her back out into the icy air of downtown Edison. "Call me, Rod! My number is on the back of the business card I gave you!"

We head to Macy's car, and she laughs as she hops into the driver's seat. "Did you get what you needed?"

"Maybe," I say, inspecting that naughty gleam in my sister's eye. "And something tells me you did, too. So does Rod stand a chance?"

"It depends."

"On what?"

"On how fast I fall in love with the Wilder brothers."

In love with the Wilder brothers.

I shake my head as we start making our way back to Cider Cove.

Macy clicks her tongue as she looks dreamily out the windshield. "Wouldn't it be something if we both ended up marrying a Wilder brother? We'd be sisters *and* we'd be sisters-in-law."

"That would be something. But it's not happening. Jasper is far too stubborn for me to hitch myself to him for life."

But then, he did ask politely for me to stay out of his way.

Maybe I'm the one who's stubborn? Not that this is surprising news to me.

But once Jasper finds out that I went to see Hannah Osmond, I doubt he'll ever want anything to do with me again.

Not that I care.

A sickening feeling boils in the pit of my stomach because something tells me I do, in fact, care.

And that begs the question—why?

16

Saturday arrives and the Harvest at the Cove Festival is finally upon us. The sun has miraculously made a reprisal, and the storm had indeed blown away from the coast. Even the ocean looks serene and cerulean today as if it too were readying for the townspeople and tourists alike to migrate down to the shoreline.

It's still early, and the vendors have yet to unpack their wares. The tables were set up at the crack of dawn, and the tents just went up an hour ago. There will be music from live bands and lots and lots of food from just about every restaurant in Cider Cove, the Cottage Inn included. And you can bet that Georgie will have all her best pieces on display this afternoon. It's bound to be a success for us all.

I glance back in the direction of the cottages, and Jasper comes to mind. I've spent the last two days avoiding him at every turn. I feel terribly guilty about breaking my word to him. But at the same time, I feel there was no other way. And truth be told, I miss him. I miss his bright eyes, his warm smile, and the way my stomach cinches tight when he steps into the vicinity. Even Fish wanted to know why her best friend, Sherlock, hadn't made a recent reprisal. I had to scoff at the thought of her referring to him as her best friend, but it was sweet nonetheless.

Aside from losing sleep over breaking my word to Jasper, my mind has been fully occupied in trying to piece together who could have possibly killed Kaitlynn. I'd come right out and ask Jasper, that is, if I believed he truly knew who the killer was—although I'm not so certain about that.

But once I got ready for the day, it hit me who might have the answer, or at least point me in the right direction. As soon as I can, I speed off in my car and head to the tract of houses just beneath the orchard to see Jeannie Branch one more time.

Of course, I called ahead and told Jeannie I was coming by, and that's exactly why she's waving me down with a smile from the driveway.

I hop out of my car and head on up to meet her.

"I can't believe you sold out of my stuff!" She hops up and down with genuine excitement. Her hair is up in a whippet of a ponytail, her cheeks look rosy, and the freckles on her nose are just as adorable as they were the first time we met.

"Yup, I sure did." And I'm thankful I don't need to lie about it. "The spa at the inn said the customers are raving about it. I guess you really are sitting on a gold mine."

"You should see my premium stuff." She wrinkles her nose over at the garage. "What the heck, I'll let you see it. My new radiance cream is going to set the world on fire."

I follow her up to the garage, and she pulls out a box from the top shelf. I remember the day I came here with Georgie; she wasn't interested in even letting us peek inside these cartons.

"Look at this." She opens the lid, exposing hundreds of small mint green colored boxes and hands me one.

"Hey"—I muse as I spot her face splashed across the side of each one of these tiny mint green wonders—"you make quite the cover model. I like that."

"Yeah, well, Kaitlynn wasn't too thrilled with it. But this cream was my baby. She thought it was too high-end. The ingredients are premium so we have to pass the buck along to the consumer. But that's just business. Anyway, I thought it would be fun to showcase a natural woman instead of hiring some perfect model who had never even heard of our products."

"How much for a box?"

"Forty a piece, but I'll give them to you for ten each. I figure you're all the advertising I've got right now."

"How about I take ten and we'll go from there?"

"Sounds good to me. And I boxed up an order identical to the one you had before. I'll help you get those to your car."

Jeannie helps me do just that, and once the trunk is closed, I decide to go for the gold myself.

"Any news on who might have killed Kaitlynn?"

"Nope." She averts her eyes. *As if that were going to happen anytime soon.* "That detective from Seaview called me a few times, but it sounds like they're up against a dead end." *He's a hottie, though. I'd go after him if I wasn't knee-deep trying to pull my life together. And who cares if he's in a relationship? I bet he's got some plain, sorry girlfriend who bores him to tears. It would be like stealing candy from a baby. Lord knows I've done it before.*

I take a breath as I try my hardest not to react to her thoughts. I've learned long ago that you can't really judge others just because they're having thoughts you disapprove of. We're all entitled to an errant thought or two, no matter how mean or disillusioned they might be.

"A dead end, huh?" I shrug her way. "Geez. I can't imagine what that must feel like for you. Have you had time to consider who you think could have done this?"

223

Jeannie closes her eyes a moment. "I don't know. Honestly, I can't fathom why anyone would do this at all."

I try to get a read on her thoughts, but there aren't any at the moment.

"How about vengeance? I heard a rumor that there was a girl in her circle who was out for blood—perhaps literally. Something to do with the rocky history of their fathers."

Her eyes widen a notch. "Who in the world would tell you that?" She sucks in a quick breath. "Oh my goodness, don't bother answering. It was Hannah, wasn't it?" She moans hard. "Leave it to that little witch to try to stir things up for poor Kaitlynn, even in death." She shudders. "Was she coming around the café?"

"Uh, yes, actually." I'm not about to fess up to driving to Edison in order to hunt her down. "She swung by the other afternoon. So, it's not true?"

"Oh, it's true." Her eyes widen with disbelief. "But it's Hannah who had the vengeance. It was her father who got screwed over and went to prison. But some people can't stop lying and scheming even after the tragic facts. Poor Kaitlynn is dead, and she's still trying to destroy her." She shakes her head at the thought. "I'd better get ready for the day. I'll be at the festival tonight. I can't wait to hear the live bands."

"Stop by my booth. I've got an apple walnut cinnamon roll with your name on it."

"You bet!" She waves as she takes off for the house and closes up the garage.

I take off for the inn, feeling more confused than I was to begin with.

17

Fall in Cider Cove is usually a sight to behold with the plethora of trees that turn every shade of ruby. The leaf peeping tours in the area bring the tourists to our corner of the world by the droves. But today, the entire world seems to have flocked to the cove for an entirely different reason.

It's almost four in the afternoon, the sun is getting ready to set, and a live band is wailing away in the distance. The throngs of people who have bundled up and come out for the event all seem to be having a wonderful time.

I've been working the Cottage Café booth with Emmie for the last three hours, and we've already had to replenish our supply of apple walnut cinnamon rolls *twice*.

"I think we need a new batch," I say to Emmie as she boxes up another dozen.

"I agree. The problem is people aren't just buying one or two. They're buying them by the box."

"You really hit this one out of the park, Emmie." I nod across the way. "It looks like Georgie is hitting it out of the park, too."

Georgie's booth has been inundated with people examining her wares. The name of her booth is Sea Glass Treasures, and I think the allure of that alone is enough to make the masses gravitate her way.

I spot a tall, dark, and handsome detective making his way over with Sherlock on a leash, and my heart leaps at the sight of him. And how I hate that he has the power to elicit such a biological response in me.

"Emmie, I'll be right back." I take off for the café, and Fish jumps by my side.

You see them, don't you? Fish sounds both concerned and excited by the prospect of seeing Jasper and Sherlock.

I glance her way and give a quick nod.

Who cares if you've been working on the case? She grows more animated by the second. *This game of keep-away you're playing is keeping me from properly exacting my vengeance on that ornery dog of his.*

"Just a few days ago he was your best friend."

Fish lets out a sharp meow as if contesting the thought, and I can't help but laugh.

"Bizzy?" a deep voice calls out from behind, and I turn to find Jasper and Sherlock on our heels.

"You're about to get your wish," I whisper to Fish just as they come upon us.

"Jasper, hello." I pull a tight smile. "I was just about to head in and pick up some more inventory for the booth. But it's nice to see you both enjoying yourselves." Fish hops from one side of me to the other as if trying to incite poor Sherlock into another battle of the claws and the fangs.

Jasper sighs heavily. "Why do I get the feeling you're avoiding me?" He offers a crooked grin. "Bizzy, if I came across too strong, I apologize for that."

But I don't regret a single kiss. He glances to my lips momentarily, and I try not to smile.

Sherlock barks over at Fish. *Bizzy, stop her. She's making me dizzy, and she knows I'm on a leash. I can't properly chase her or I'll be reprimanded.*

I lean over and give Sherlock a quick pat between the ears.

"You didn't come on too strong," I say, meeting up with Jasper's eyes once again. "I'm just overwhelmed with the inn and now the festival." I swallow hard, hoping I won't regret what comes next. "So, have you solved the case? Is Kaitlynn's killer behind bars?"

His brows pinch in the middle. ***Is she mocking me? She has to know I would have told her if I made an arrest.***

"No." He takes a moment to examine me. "But we're close. I should have news for you soon."

"Oh? What is it that you know?" I lean in and bear hard into his eyes. For some reason, I've found that looking someone in the eye usually sponsors an entire litany of thoughts to bubble to the surface. But, apparently, not with him.

I'm met with nothing but silence.

Jasper frowns momentarily. "Don't worry about it tonight. You've got enough on your plate."

"You wouldn't happen to know if someone had a vendetta out against Kaitlynn or her family, would you?"

His left eye comes shy of winking, and a bite of heat crosses my stomach.

Not fair.

That little facial twitch made him look far more devastatingly handsome than he already is.

"Who did you talk to?" he asks and in a not-so friendly manner, mind you.

"I didn't talk to anyone." I'm quick to take umbrage with his tone even if I am playing fast and loose with the truth.

Fish jumps in front of me. ***Don't worry, Bizzy. I know how to get rid of them for you.*** She reaches out and swipes her paw at Sherlock's nose, but Jasper cinches the leash, assuring us that the poor pooch isn't going anywhere.

"Bizzy?" I can practically see Jasper's wheels turning. "You spoke to someone, didn't you?"

My mouth opens to contest the idea, but I can't seem to bring myself to shed another lie. "Maybe?"

"Bizzy." He squeezes his eyes shut tight for a moment. "You realize these could be potentially dangerous people. You don't know what you're up against. You can't keep putting yourself out there like that. One person is already dead. And I don't want the body count to rise."

"Why would the killer come after me? For asking a couple of questions?"

"Yes." He nods with an incredulous look on his face. "That is precisely why. Whoever did this has to be desperately afraid of being caught. And desperate people are capable of doing anything. Committing a second homicide is certainly not off the table. Bizzy, who did you speak with?"

My mouth opens then closes.

"Was it Hannah?" His brows hike a notch.

I bite down hard on my lower lip as Sherlock does his best to swat his paws over at Fish.

"It was Hannah," Jasper growls it out with disappointment resonating in his tone.

"Okay, fine, it was Hannah. But my sister was with me. And, if you must know, Macy is in the process of getting hot and heavy with the owner of The Rat Tat. It's not my fault Hannah just so happened to be there while we were paying a visit." I feel smaller than an inch for spilling so many questionable half-truths at his feet.

He tips his head to the side as if to contest every word that just came from my mouth. As he should.

"Fine," I concede with regret. "I went looking for her. But aren't you in the least bit impressed I knew where to find her?"

"No," he flatlines.

"Well, I don't care. She told me this bizarre story about how Kaitlynn's father partook in some criminal activity, and then his buddies both went to prison with him even though they were innocent. And she alluded that one of the men had a daughter who later befriended Kaitlynn. But she wouldn't say who. So, when I spoke to Jeannie this morning, she all but balked at the—"

"You spoke to Jeannie this morning?" His brows frame his face in a straight line. "Bizzy, you promised me that you would not take this further."

"No, those were your words. And why do you keep insisting that I stay out of this? I thought we already

231

determined that Kaitlynn was my friend." My voice hikes an octave without meaning to.

"You admitted to hardly knowing the girl." His voice is right there, hiking in agitation to meet with mine.

Fish hops onto Sherlock's back, and Jasper steps to the side as the two of them begin to snarl and yowl as they wrestle it out.

"Fish!" I howl at her, but she's proving unstoppable.

Both Jasper and I do our best to wrestle them apart but to no avail. Sherlock flips Fish over like a seasoned wrestler and pins my poor kitty to the sand.

Bizzy! Fish cries out, but if I didn't know better, it almost sounded as if she were laughing.

Sherlock lands his mouth over her, and Fish lets out a yodeling cry. I quickly snatch her from his jaw and hold her tight.

Sherlock looks up my way. ***Sorry, Bizzy. I couldn't help myself. She started it.***

I shoot Jasper a look.

Why is she scowling at me? Jasper's brows bounce as if he were perplexed. ***Why is she always angry with me? What doesn't she get about the fact she's putting herself in harm's way? She's too stubborn for her own good.***

I suck in a quick breath.

"I know what you're thinking. I'm not stubborn." I don't mind one bit calling him out on it. "And before you start in with all the good reasons you have for me to stay away from the case, know that this is a free country and I can still see and speak to whomever I wish."

He narrows his eyes my way. **Two can play hardball**. "This might be a free country, but there are laws that its citizens need to abide by. I can have you arrested if you meddle in this case any more than you already have."

"Oh my goodness. Are you threatening me?"

Sherlock whimpers as he lands his paws over his eyes. *Bizzy, don't test him. When he's firm, he's firm.*

Jasper leans in, those silver eyes of his flashing like lightning. "No, Bizzy, that's not a threat. That's a promise."

A breath hitches in my throat as I inch back a notch.

"How dare you," I seethe. "I believe we're done, detective. I don't take kindly to being spoken to that way."

His eyes widen a notch. ***Being spoken to that way? It's the law. And more than that, I don't want anything to happen to her.*** He looks genuinely stymied.

At least he's not overtly trying to be a jerk.

He frowns my way. "Look, you don't have to like what I'm saying to you. But you do have to obey the laws. Approach one more suspect, and I'm taking you in."

"On what grounds?"

233

"On obstruction of justice."

I suck in a quick breath at his audacity. "You should be taken in for obstructing justice. You're the one who's dragging his feet. You said you were close to making an arrest, and I've yet to see evidence of this."

"I don't owe you evidence." A smile twitches on his lips, and it only frustrates me all the more.

"You're right," I say, taking a moment to memorize that determined look on his face and it breaks my heart all the more. "And I don't owe you anything either. It was nice meeting up, Detective Wilder," the words thump out of me with sorrow. "Maybe we should stay out of one another's way from here on out since we have such a difficult time seeing eye to eye. Not to mention the fact I don't look so good in silver bracelets. Enjoy the rest of your time at the inn. If you need anything, I'll be happy to make certain all of your needs are met—that is, if you don't arrest me first." I stalk off toward the café without bothering to look back.

Perhaps some people are best forgotten.

Now if I can only forget about those kisses.

The night wears on, and the population on the beach only seems to grow. Emmie and I can't keep up with the crowd. And in about an hour we'll run out of apple walnut cinnamon rolls altogether.

Melissa and Topher Montgomery, who own and operate the orchard, come our way. Melissa is a sweet brunette with wild curly hair and a wide smile that never leaves her face. And Topher is a tall, gentle giant with the warmest brown eyes you will ever see. His family has owned the orchard for as long as I can remember.

"Your cinnamon rolls are on the house," I say as I quickly box up half a dozen. "If it wasn't for the fresh apples from your orchard, they wouldn't taste near as good."

Melissa laughs. "Our pumpkins promise to be just as delicious."

Topher nods. "We're coming up on our busiest season yet, and we're looking to kick it off with a party next Saturday."

Melissa nods. "We'll be hosting the Haunted Harvest Festival at the pumpkin patch and we're expecting quite a crowd. We were hoping we could have the café donate some light appetizers and desserts to have on hand for the opening. We're asking every restaurant in and out of Cider Cove in hopes we'll have more than enough to feed the hungry crowds on kickoff day."

"Say no more. We would love to do it. It's our pleasure."

"Great." Topher takes the box from Emmie. "And, in exchange, I'll have someone bring over a load of pumpkins to decorate the inn with."

"That would be wonderful. I just know the guests would love it."

No sooner do they take off than Emmie's eyes widen as she looks at something just over my shoulder. And before I can sneak a peek myself, she pulls me close, in one aggressive move.

"What is it?" I try to glance back, but she dances me to the left.

"Nothing. Nothing at all." Her dark hair catches the twinkle lights and glistens in long, glossy waves.

"Emmie." I laugh as I wiggle free before turning around, and a hard groan expels from me at the sight. "Dear Lord. She doesn't waste any time, does she?"

There she is, Mayor Mackenzie Man-Eater Woods, cozying up to the questionable detective. Poor Sherlock looks as if he's bored out of his mind, but Jasper seems to be nodding intently at whatever nonsense she's telling him.

Traitor.

Mack catches my eye and offers me a quick wave, prompting Jasper to turn this way.

"Oh no, you don't," I say, spinning around as I pretend to busy myself by straightening the counter. "You know what, Emmie? I think I'm going to trot over and see how Georgie is doing. Do you mind?"

"I don't mind one bit." She pulls me in and presses those pale blue eyes into mine. "I'm so sorry, Bizzy."

"Don't be. He just wasn't the one for me." My gut wrenches when I say it as if calling me out on the lie.

Emmie is already privy to everything that went down between Jasper and me a little while ago. As soon as I got back to the booth, I spilled everything to her. I've never been one to keep anything from Emmie—aside from that tiny quirk that lends me the ability to pry into other people's thoughts. There are just some things people shouldn't be privy to—and I'm talking about reading minds. I know for a fact it would change everything between us, and in no way would I ever want that.

I drudge my way through the sand, through the crowds, as I make my way to Georgie's booth and bump into a body, nearly knocking the drinks right out of their hands.

"I'm so sorry!" I say, looking up, only to be met with a friendly face. "Chris!" I say with a touch of too much excitement. "It's nice to see you out and about."

Chris Davidson looks clean-shaven with a smile spreading over his face as he lifts the beers in his hands my way.

"It's nice to see you, too, Bizzy. My friends insisted I come out." He glances toward the café. "I didn't think I could do it. But they said it would be good for me to push past the pain. We're having a small memorial for Kaitlynn tomorrow, right here on the beach at noon. You're welcome to come. Please invite any of Kaitlynn's co-workers. It would be an honor to have them."

"That's very kind. Thank you." I frown past him, knowing full well Detective Wilder might be barreling his way over to arrest *me* of all people. A thought comes to me. "Hey, Chris? The night Kaitlynn was killed she had a very fancy ring with her. She wasn't wearing it. She was putting it in her purse." Okay, so I didn't exactly see her put it in her purse, but that's close enough.

Chris glances around a moment. *A ring? Crap.* He looks my way.

"Yes, I know all about it." He gives a long blink. "That was an engagement ring, or a promise ring, or some sort of commitment jewelry her boyfriend gave her."

"Her boyfriend?" I'm not sure I heard him right.

"I guess there's no harm in telling you. But I think she and Cameron got back together about a month before she was killed."

"Cameron?" I blink back, surprised.

"I'm pretty sure about it." He nods. "I think it started off innocent enough—complaining about me, I'm sure. But then, I heard things were heating up between her and someone, and she needed to make a decision. Apparently, she was about to break things off with me that night."

"I'm sorry. That must have been hard to hear."

He takes a full breath. "Not as hard as you think. We were having trouble." He winces as he looks out at the sand. "I was seeing someone around the same time, too. Only I wasn't about to break it off with Kaitlynn. I had just cut things off with the other girl that night. I was going to try to win Kate back. I'd give anything for that to still be possible. She never really loved Cam. She liked the idea of him. What she didn't like was how I was acting. I guess there are some things that I'll have to live with—and the guilt I feel about this is smothering."

"Chris." I glance back in the direction his eyes keep shooting off to. "Who is this other woman?" Could it be Hannah?

He shakes his head. "It's over. It's not important. Have a great rest of the night, Bizzy." He takes off, and I'm breathless at what he's just revealed.

Whoever this woman is, she might be the killer. Chris dumped her. He was hoping to get back with Kaitlynn. This mystery woman certainly had the motive to pull off a crime of passion.

I make my way to Georgie's booth.

"Bizzy!" She tosses her hands in the air. "Look at my table!"

I glance down, and there's not a single item left gracing its surface.

"You've been pillaged?"

"No! I sold out! Can you believe it?"

"Yes, I believe it. Because I believe in you."

"Bizzy." She leans across the way and captures my cheeks in her hands. "You are an angel. Without your encouragement, and the free rent doesn't hurt either, I was able to accomplish my dreams tonight."

A dull laugh pumps through me. "You don't have free rent, Georgie. You're three months behind." And I'm covering for her. "But I'm thrilled all of your dreams were met tonight by selling your priceless works of art. You deserve all the success in the world."

She waves me off. "I'm not talking about that. I'm talking about the fact that Mayor Stick-Up-Her-Rear-Woods asked me to work on a beautification project right here on Main Street. You know that retaining wall at the end of the street that keeps the art center from tumbling to the ground? The city is paying to have an artist lay a mosaic over the front of it. And do you know who that artist is?"

"Macy?" I can't help but tease her.

"No—it's *me*! Can you believe it? I have to go and celebrate. I hear the Unchained Bistro has brought tapas, and I'm on a hunt for a decent margarita to go with them. And don't think I've forgotten about you," she says, cinching her purse over her shoulder. "I'll stop by and pick up a cinnamon roll for dessert. But not if you charge me." She playfully wags her finger my way. "I'm a starving artist, remember? It's not good for my brand for me to walk around with money." She takes off, and a laugh gets locked in my throat. At least something is working out for someone tonight, and I'm glad it's Georgie.

I glance back toward the café where I saw the malfeasance taking place, but both Mack and Jasper are nowhere to be seen.

Great.

They probably got a room.

Better yet, they hightailed it to his cottage, and now poor Sherlock will have to witness the unholy coital event. Just the thought of Mack attacking Jasper that way makes my stomach boil with rage.

I set out in the opposite direction and stumble upon a welcome sight for sore eyes, my mother.

"Mom!" I wrap my arms around her tight. "I'm so glad you could come."

"Are you kidding? I wouldn't miss it. In fact, I'm glad I didn't." She takes a sip from her fruity cocktail. Mom looks impossibly gorgeous tonight in a pair of jeans and a red cable knit sweater with a white blouse underneath with the collar popped circa 1983. Mom has never quite parted with her preppy ways, or her feathered hair, and yet she's never once looked outdated. She doesn't look nearly her age. In fact, people have often mistaken her for my sister than they ever have my mother. And it's always a genuine sentiment. I should know. I've confirmed it by way of their thoughts.

"I'm glad you're here for sure. Have you seen Macy?"

"No, I was a bit preoccupied." She leans in and gives a little wink. "Met a boy."

"What?" My mouth falls open with the quasi-salacious news. "Do tell."

"His name is Maximus, and get this. He owns a restaurant named after himself down in Seaview."

The smile quickly fades from my face. "*Maximus*?"

"I know—it's a wild name. But you'll never guess what his last name is—Wilder! Isn't that well, *wild*?" She laughs and looks the happiest I've seen her in months.

Dear Lord. That's Jasper's brother! This can't be right. I can't be dating Jasper while she sees Maximus. That goes against the laws of nature or something.

And then it occurs to me that I just cut Jasper out of my life rather abruptly tonight, and I'm filled with anguish.

Great. My mother is going to fall in love and marry his brother, and I'll be forced to see Jasper and his new bride Mack on every major holiday. I can't wait for this new, psychotic leg of my life to begin.

"Anyway"—Mom beams—"he gave me his number. We're going out for drinks tomorrow night. Don't say anything, but he's just a wee bit younger than me. I may have lied about my age," she says that last bit through the side of her mouth.

"You mean he had the audacity to ask?"

"Heavens no. I always volunteer it because I can almost read their minds. I know they're wondering."

A weak smile comes and goes. Macy won't be too thrilled, but such is life.

"I'd better go." She checks her phone. "I'm volunteering at the Lather and Light booth so Macy can prowl the grounds. I really hope she meets a nice young man soon herself. But it just seems like all the good ones are taken." She stalks off sipping her drink.

"I know what Macy would say. All the good ones are taken—by her mother."

I pull out my phone as Kaitlynn's murder begins to take over my thoughts once again.

Fish appears, bounding down from the café, and together we walk off to the right until we're past the booths and the thick of the bodies milling around, pressing against one another as if it were a free-for-all.

"Oh, Fish"—I bend over and scoop her up—"I wish I knew who Chris was sleeping with. I think that might be the key to everything." I pull out my phone and look at those pictures I took of the contents of Kaitlynn's purse.

The library receipt with a slew of business books. The ring that glittered like mad as if it had its own secret to tell, and, boy, did it ever. A trio of receipts lined up stare blankly at me, and I enlarge each one—pizza, one for Thaime for Thai, and one for less than a hundred dollars marked Bowden Development. Bowden—why does that sound familiar? That's right, the shipping labels at Natural Beauty had the same name.

A thought comes to me, and I do a quick search of Bowden Development on my phone. Nothing but some general ads for the company and a few reviews here and there. And then I scroll farther.

"Oh my goodness." I glance up at the crowd sweltering in the distance. "I know who the killer is."

18

The sound of the surf pounding the shoreline is far more soothing than the sound of the live band that happens to be screaming into the mic at the moment.

Fish and I weave our way back into the crowd where I spot Chris and his friends standing near the waterline, each with a drink in their hand, laughter in their throat.

Within their circle, I spot Cameron speaking with a girl about my age.

I can't blame him for having a conversation with someone, but the way he's leering at her, the way his hand is riding down her hip, it sure doesn't look as if he's mourning Kaitlynn too hard—that is, if they were getting back together. According to Cameron, they were still friends. But Chris did say she had a boyfriend.

Speaking of Chris, he doesn't look as if he's mourning Kaitlynn too hard either, but at least he's not pawing Sammy. That's who he's currently locked in a conversation with.

That night comes back to me in snatches. Both Chris and Sammy were acting strange. But Sammy was the one talking about Kaitlynn in the past tense before it was ever revealed to her that Kaitlynn was dead. It does make me wonder if my theory is correct.

Chris was acting funny, too. He had some drunk blonde pawing all over him, and he sure didn't seem to mind. Then I distinctly remember him nodding at someone in the crowd as the sirens cut through the air. It was almost as if he were signaling them or acknowledging what the sirens could have meant.

I spot Hannah standing off to the side, talking with a few girls, and her blonde hair flashes in the moonlight. A memory comes to me from the night of Kaitlynn's murder. That drunk blonde in Chris' lap. It was her. And oddly enough, Chris wasn't pawing all over her. Hannah did insist Chris was seeing someone and that it wasn't her. I suppose it could still be true.

And just beyond her I see Jeannie Branch and Rissa in what looks to be a heated conversation.

Huh. That's funny. It almost looks as if they're having the same heated argument Rissa and Kaitlynn were having the night she was killed. Maybe that's a personality quirk of Rissa's? Maybe she's a loud and animated talker? Or maybe she's just hard to get along with. She does seem to be the constant in the equation.

Fish rubs up against my chin. ***Don't you think we should be getting back to the stand? I have a bad feeling about this, Bizzy. Maybe that obnoxious detective was right. The last thing we want is to get involved with someone dangerous.***

"There are a million people here tonight. I doubt I'm in any danger at all."

Weren't there a million people here the night poor Kaitlynn was murdered?

"All right, smarty paws. Point proven." I decide to walk by Kaitlynn's beautiful and polished friends, and sure enough not one of them seems to notice me. And why would they? They're all too busy having a great time. I'm sure Kaitlynn would have wanted it that way. She was a sweet soul. I didn't need to know her for a year to figure that out.

Rissa and Jeannie hit the crescendo of their argument, and they both stalk off in opposite directions at once like a couple of balls on the pool table that were just hit with force.

Rissa takes off toward Sammy and Chris, but Jeannie makes a dash toward the boulders that lead to the woods.

It's quiet out that way and the perfect place to think—or the perfect place to sulk after an argument.

"Jeannie," I call out and quickly catch up to her.

She turns and offers a bleak smile my way. "Oh hi, Bizzy. I was about to visit your booth. But I had a nasty run-in with a friend. Lucky for you, I like to eat my feelings. I'll take two dozen of those cinnamon rolls, and I'm not kidding."

"That bad, huh?"

A dull laugh pumps from her as she gives Fish a quick pat.

"It was, but it's over now. I'm pretty good at letting things slide off my back. I like to save my revenge for later." She gives a wicked grin.

I swallow hard. "Jeannie, your father, his last name is different than yours. Can I ask why?"

Her eyes widen a moment. "He went to prison." She shrugs. "It wasn't his fault, but I don't even bother telling people that anymore. No one believes me. They say, 'Sure, everyone in prison is innocent. Isn't that what they all say?'" She rolls her eyes, and they flash in the dark.

"It was Kaitlynn's father who did the crime, wasn't it?"

Her mouth falls open. "You know? I didn't think anyone knew that."

"Yes, I know. You mentioned you were new to Cider Cove. But Kaitlynn knew who you were."

248

She shakes her head. "We moved here. Kaitlynn's family is from Rose Glen. We never talked about it. She never wanted it to affect our friendship."

"But it did. How could it not? Is that why you went after Chris?"

Jeannie inches back as if I slapped her. "What?" ***How does she know that? And what else could she possibly know?***

Fish lets out a growling meow. ***She's frightened. Let's get back, Bizzy. We're too far from the crowd. I don't feel safe out here with her.***

Fish sprints out of my arms and darts between my ankles.

My adrenaline kicks in as Jeannie takes a full step back and I close in on her.

"You killed her, didn't you? Chris broke it off with you that night. Is that why you did it? He wanted to go back to her. He chose her over you." My panting becomes wild as I lock eyes with her. "Jeannie, this was clearly a crime of passion. I'm sure you were overwhelmed at the moment. An insanity plea could work for you."

Her chest bucks, her face grows strangely blank and her eyes vacant as if she were reliving that awful night.

"I didn't mean to do it. She was arguing with Rissa"— her voice grows tight and angry—"over that stupid, stupid boyfriend of theirs."

"Of *theirs*?"

"Yes." She gives a caustic nod. "That's who Kaitlynn was seeing. She was seeing Ben."

"Not Cameron?"

My goodness. Chris knew she was seeing someone else. He assumed it was Cameron. He was wrong. And that night of her death—Kaitlynn told me it was a friend of hers dating Rissa's boyfriend. And if Jeannie is right, Kaitlynn herself was that friend. Of course, she wouldn't admit it.

A husky laugh comes from Jeannie. "Chris was her cover. Chris became whatever lie she needed to plug a hole, and he was always up for a game. He still loved her. But so did Ben. He even gave Kate a ring." She gets a far-off look in her eyes once again. "Rissa knew that someone close to her was the problem. She just didn't know how close. I told her tonight. She hated Kaitlynn for a number of reasons, but she still didn't believe me. I don't even know why I bothered. But Kaitlynn came up in our conversation, and I thought she'd want the truth. Do you want to know what the irony is? Kaitlynn decided at the last minute not to break up with Chris. On the night she died, once Rissa took off and I had a moment alone with Kaitlynn, she told me she couldn't go through with it. She wasn't going to break up with Chris after all. She said she could tell something was changing inside him, and maybe, just maybe, their love stood a chance. She was leaving Ben. She called him a mistake."

"And that's where the rage came from." I nod as I say it. "Kaitlynn was holding the knife, wasn't she? It belonged to the inn. It was from a table she was bussing. Your pent-up rage from what her father did to yours, in addition to the thought of Chris and Kaitlynn reuniting, pushed you to the brink. It only makes sense. You were blind with rage—you were alone with her, and you killed her."

"I wasn't alone with Kaitlynn." She looks past me into the crowd. "Sammy saw everything."

"What? Sammy witnessed it?" My heart riots clear up into my ears, detonating with every beat. "Of course, she did. That's why she spoke about Kaitlynn in past tense the night she was murdered."

"She saw." Jeannie nods as if she were coming to. "She didn't know how bad Kate's injuries were until later, but she wanted to stay out of it. She wanted to let us deal with things on our own. Sammy has never been one to get her hands dirty. She asked me to confess. I told her I would, but one day turned into two, and then a week went by and here we are. I thought I might actually get away with it. But that's not the case, is it?" Her eyes ignite with fury.

"Jeannie, you didn't even bring the murder weapon with you that night. There's still time to go to the sheriff's department and turn yourself in. I can go with you if you like. This wasn't premeditated."

"No, it wasn't." Her eyes dart to mine, cold and dangerous. "And neither was this."

Jeannie grabs ahold of my arms and throws me down to the boulders, sending the back of my head against the rock with a thump.

Fish lets out a riotous roar and tries to jump between us, but Jeannie grabs my shoulders once again and does her best to beat my head against the granite.

My vision blurs. I see stars, and not the ones overhead. It takes everything in me to latch onto her shirt and give a firm shove to her chest. I pull myself upright, and I fight—I wrestle her right over the damp sand as a wave slaps down over the two of us, hard.

"Oh no!" A horrific cry comes from me as I struggle to get away from the water.

Fish lets out another howling roar before darting off in the sand. And I won't lie. My heart sinks at the prospect of being alone out here in the dark, too far from the crowd for anyone to hear or see us.

Another wave lands over us, and this one drags us off with it as it surges back to sea. Please, anything but this. Struggle as I might, Jeannie won't let go. Instead, she does her best to hold me under as we bob and weave in the restless sea.

"Stop it!" I howl in her face as we come up for air, her fingernails digging into my neck as she struggles to pull me under the water once again. "You don't have to do this!"

"I'm sorry, Bizzy." She pulls me farther into the ocean as her body trembles hard from the icy brine and it's as if she's having a seizure. "I'll make it look like an accident." She submerges my face into the water and lies over my back as if she were using me as a floatation device. That day, all those years ago in the whiskey barrel, comes back to me and it's as if Mack herself is holding me down once again.

I struggle to grab ahold of her as my body does its best to twist to safety, but Jeannie proves immovable.

Can't breathe. Can't hold my breath another moment longer.

Bizzy!

I buck as I hear an all too familiar voice.

Hold on!

It's Sherlock.

I buck and writhe in what just might be my final moments.

I need air.

Just one breath.

It's too painful to deny myself the pleasure of breathing. Taking in a lungful of water would be better than this. And I'm about to do just that when her hold on me loosens and I cork to the surface, coughing and sputtering.

"*Bizzy*!"

I turn to find Jasper running this way and Sherlock attached to the back of Jeannie's shirt by his teeth.

Jasper quickly subdues her and has her in handcuffs. He puts in a call, and in no time a swarm of deputies surround us.

"She did it," I gasp, staggering my way over to the nearest boulder. "She confessed. She killed Kaitlynn Zimmerman."

"Bizzy." Jasper pulls me in, wrapping his arms around me tight. "What were you thinking?" He leans back. "This is exactly why I didn't want you running after a sus—"

I pull him down by the neck and crash my mouth to his, landing a heartfelt kiss of gratitude right over his lips. Jasper softens to me, moaning as our kiss becomes something less than chaste, and we indulge in something far headier than I could have ever hoped for.

We part ways, and I bat my lashes up at him and shrug.

"I couldn't think of a better way to keep you from lecturing me."

A crooked grin ignites over his face. "I like your methods. And do you know what else I like?" His finger brushes over my cheek. "You, warm and dry." He takes off his jacket and lands it around my shoulders, and I stop shivering for just a moment. "Truce?"

"Truce," I say, wrapping my arms around his waist. "Please tell me, right now, if you have any plans on seeing Mayor Woods. Because if you do, I'll have to bow out graciously. I'm not interested in the drama she brings to the table."

He shakes his head. "She's not my type."

"Oh? You have a type?" I can't help but be amused—and elated to hear it.

"Yes, in fact, I do. About yea tall." He lands his hand to the top of my head. "Gorgeous blue eyes, dark hair, lips that I can't get my mind off of. Feisty. Maybe a teeny bit stubborn—but challenging, and I like a good challenge." He takes a quick breath. "And full disclosure, Mayor Woods offered me drinks at her place, and I declined. Now that was not a challenge. And even if it was, it would have been the wrong one." He dots another kiss to my lips. "I'm not in the least bit interested in Mayor Woods. I'm interested in you, Bizzy."

"What a coincidence," I say, my gaze unable to look away from those magnetic silver eyes. "I'm interested in you."

Jasper bows down to kiss me just as Sherlock barks into the night, and we glance that way to find Fish nestled beside him as if warming herself against his fur.

We share a laugh at the two of them, and Jasper ticks his head to the side.

"It's funny"—he says—"this is exactly where it all began."

My mouth falls open. "You're right. This is where we met. And on that day you were equally as soaked. But no need to reprise that."

"How about we start a new tradition? Warm cider and a fire at my place? I also have to question you and take a full report of tonight's incident."

"Only if I can get a shower and my sweats on beforehand."

"Sounds like a good deal."

The deputies take Jeannie in, and Jasper takes me back to his place for questioning.

And I start each answer with a kiss.

19

The Country Cottage Café is brimming with people. It's the final Saturday of September, and fall is in full swing. The inn is nearly booked to capacity once again, and it seems everyone in Cider Cove is breathing a little easier now that Kaitlynn's killer is behind bars.

Jeannie was booked and charged with second-degree murder. And Sammy was implicated in trying to help conceal a homicide. They've both secured top-notch lawyers, and the rest is entirely up to our legal system.

Jasper and Sherlock enter the café, and my heart skips a beat for the both of them. Jasper has on his jeans and a sweater and looks as if he's ready to cozy up next to a fire. And if I get my way, I'll be right there to cozy up with him.

Bizzy! Sherlock barks. ***Where's Fish? I've got a bone to pick with her. She usually jumps out of the***

***bushes as soon as I leave the cottage, and she
wasn't there to greet me properly this morning.***

I wrinkle my nose at the adorable pooch as I lean over the counter. "Well, hello there, Inspector Sherlock. I bet you're wondering where Fish is. She's outside on the patio just waiting to pop out and greet you."

Sherlock jumps and barks while looking at his owner, and Jasper laughs.

"It's almost as if he understood you." He lifts a brow my way, and I lean across the counter and land a kiss right over his lips. "I'll have Sherlock save me a seat outside, and I'll be right back to put in an order."

"I'll be right here waiting."

Mom, my sister, and Georgie wander in, bundled in sweaters and scarves. Macy has a fantastic pair of boots on that I lent her a few years back. Wait a minute. Did I lend those to her? I'm starting to think Macy has gone shopping in my closet one too many times.

"Guess what?" Macy grins so hard it's practically electric. Normally, this wouldn't faze me, but considering the source of that brimming smile, I'm a touch worried about whatever might pop from her mouth next. "Mom is finally bringing her mystery man around, and we'll get to meet him in the flesh!"

An entire stream of words gets trapped in my throat. "Really?" I lift a brow my mother's way, and she gives a sly nod.

I made my mother promise she wouldn't say a word to Macy regarding the fact she was dating Jasper's brother. In fact, I haven't said a word to Jasper—in part due to the fact I was certain it would never last.

It's not going to last. Right?

A mild sense of panic grips me. "When is this miracle going to take place?"

Mom leans in. "This Saturday. His restaurant was one of many that was asked to cater the Haunted Harvest Festival being held at the orchard. I'm going to help him make the delivery and set everything up. And rumor has it, he wants to take me on a haunted hayride." She's quick to wave it off with a smile.

Macy looks as if she can hardly catch her breath. "Do you see this, Bizzy? Mom has a date on a haunted hayride. And who do I have to spook me properly? This is precisely why I need you to introduce me to those Wilder brothers."

Jasper pops up just in time, and Georgie makes wild eyes at me. "Here's one now, Bizzy. You'd better put your mark on him before Macy goes for the kill." She winks over at poor Jasper who looks mildly concerned and with good reason.

ADDISON MOORE & BELLAMY BLOOM

"Speak of the devil." Macy turns his way. "Rumor has it, you have not one but three eligible bachelors in your family." She pulls at a blonde lock of hair while batting her lashes up at him. "How soon can I meet these brothers of yours? And do you have photos and phone numbers I can have in the meantime?"

Jasper's cheek bounces with a brief smile. "One of them is dating." He shrugs. "I hear it's some hot woman from Cider Cove." He tips his head toward Macy. "It's not you, is it?"

Mom clears her throat and shakes her head my way in the event I was about to spill her secret. Little does she know I'd go to the ends of the earth to protect it. I'm not exactly thrilled we're dating brothers. And add Macy to the mix? This could get ugly.

A choking sound emits from my sister's throat. "No, it's not me—but it will be. And don't think for a minute I can't swipe that man right out of the hands of that hottie from Cider Cove. I've got a few tricks up my seductive sleeves yet. So, cough 'em up. Hey, I know! Invite them to the Haunted Harvest Festival this Saturday. There will be plenty of food and it's super casual. They don't need to stay all day. Once I've made my selection, the other two are free to go on their merry way." She offers him a scheming grin and my stomach churns, because once Macy gets her mind made up about something, there is no turning back for any of us.

"I will." Jasper shrugs my way. "I think Max mentioned something about catering the event, so you'll get to meet one of them for sure. He's the taken one, but I'll get the others to show up in support of him. And I'll get my sister to come out." He looks over at me. "I know she's anxious to meet you."

"*Ooh.*" Georgie does an odd little tap-dance. "Hear that, Bizzy? The family is anxious to meet you." She looks back his way and shoots him the stink eye. "How about your mother? When does she get to meet the parents?"

Jasper grimaces a moment. "Funny you should ask. Bizzy, I was just about to speak with you about that." He glances to the peanut gallery. "My mother's townhouse flooded. She's currently in a hotel near her home but needs something a little more permanent, and she refuses to impose on her children. Believe me, we've tried."

"Oh no, I don't have any cottages available at the moment, but I have a room right here at the inn I could lease to her for as long as she needs it."

"That would be great." There's a gleam in his eyes that says so much more. "I can't wait for you to meet her, Bizzy. She's paid up at the hotel until Saturday, so I'll help her move then."

"Perfect!"

Emmie waves from the register as my mom, sister, and Georgie head over to put in their orders.

Jasper leans in. "I owe you. How about dinner tonight? Chinese sound good?"

"It depends. Can we do takeout at my place? I'm picturing a fire and not a lot of distractions."

His lips curve with wicked intent, and my night suddenly looks far more promising than I could have predicted.

A man steps up to the counter, and Jasper does a double take in his direction. And just like that, his friendly demeanor does a rather abrupt disappearing act.

"Leo." Jasper's shoulders widen as if he were suddenly about to tackle the guy.

"Can I help you?" I look to the man. He's tall, textbook handsome, dark wavy hair, and dark eyes that look as if they don't give away his secrets.

Jasper glowers at the man. "Bizzy, this is Deputy Granger from down at the sheriff's department. We were good friends up until recently."

"Oh," I tip my head back knowingly. This must be the guy that his ex took off with.

"Just Leo." He holds out a hand my way, and I shake it. "My aunt was at the crafts fair at the cove the other night. She said she met with a woman who sold her a mosaic vase. She mentioned the woman lived on the premises. I'm hoping you can help me out. It's pertinent that I speak with her."

"Oh, that's Georgie. She's right over there in the kaftan." I'm quick to point her out. "Let me guess. She sold the vase that she keeps her life savings in again?" I try to laugh it off in an effort to lighten the mood between them, but neither is budging.

He looks right at me, his dark eyes narrowing over mine. *It's not you, is it?* He sweeps my features as if looking for a response, and I freeze. *Rumor has it, someone here at the inn can read minds.* His lips twitch with a smile. *And I'm determined to find out exactly who it is.* He looks my way. *I just want you to know that if you can hear me*—he bears hard into my eyes—*I can hear you, too.*

He takes a breath and nods at the two of us before taking off in Georgie's direction.

"Oh my goodness," I pant as I pick up a stale cup of coffee left on the counter and head that way myself. "Georgie? This kind man would like to speak with you!" I trip over my own feet, hoping that it looked like a genuine fumble, and spill the coffee along the front of her dress. "Oh goodness. If I had a dozen donuts every time I did that, I'd be happy." I glance his way. "Just one moment. I'll mop her up and bring her right back." I drag Georgie off to the tiny office inside the kitchen and seal the door shut behind us.

"Are you crazy?" I hiss as she grabs an errant apron off the desk and begins mopping herself off.

"I believe that would be you, missy. And since when do you serve cold coffee? If you're going to douse me, at least let me get a burn out of it so I can sue you properly."

"Never mind that. Georgie, why did you tell someone at the crafts fair that I can read minds?"

Her mouth rounds out in a perfect O. "Well, I didn't mean to. The woman practically dragged it out of me when she bragged that her nephew knows exactly what she's thinking. We were talking about clothing, by the way, of which you just ruined mine."

"That's just great because her nephew is here, and it looks as if he's trying to collect on some supernatural debt. *Georgie*, you can't let him know that I can read minds. You have to tell him you were kidding. That it was some guest who has long since left the inn. No one can know of my ability. He's a deputy. That's just one degree of separation from some paranormal government sponsored agency."

"Oh, I don't think you qualify as paranormal. You just have a nifty little ability there." She wiggles her fingers at me with a goofy grin on her face as if she were trying to amuse an infant. "But, of course, I'm not talking to a G-man or deputy or anyone from outer space for that matter. I'll get this straightened out, Bizzy—just you wait and see. I'll fix everything."

And that's exactly what I'm afraid of.

We head back out together, and Jasper is still there waiting for me. Emmie is manning the register, so I hop his way and we watch the fall-out together.

Georgie says a few seemingly innocent words to Leo, and he nods politely before heading back this way.

"Leo." Jasper nods to him. "What's going on?"

He looks to Jasper and shakes his head. "Just running an errand for my aunt. It looks like everything is squared away. She wasn't sure if she paid for the piece she picked up and couldn't sleep. I told her I'd check it out. Turns out, she did."

I shake my head at him. *Nice cover.*

He turns my way. *Thank you.*

My eyes enlarge at his response. No matter how hard I try to control it, I'm physically stunned into submission.

Leo tips his head back my way, a smile twitching on his lips. *It's you, isn't it? Bizzy, I'm here to help you. Trust me. I know the answers to the questions you have. I'll be back. But, in the meantime, you know where to find me.*

He nods to Jasper. "It was nice seeing you again." He pats him on the back before looking my way. "And it was nice meeting you."

He takes off, and I let out an enormous breath I didn't even realize I was holding.

Jasper leans in until he hooks my attention. "Bizzy, are you all right?"

"I'm fine. Everything is going to be just fine." I force a smile because a part of me demands to believe it.

That night, Jasper and I eat takeout in my living room until we're stuffed. We curl up next to a roaring fire and sip hot cider as we watch Sherlock and Fish bat at one another playfully until Fish curls against Sherlock's belly and they both fall asleep.

I look up at Jasper and whisper, "They're so sweet."

"You know what else is sweet?" His bright eyes siren at me with the brilliance of twin moons. "You."

Jasper lands a kiss to my lips that starts off achingly slow before morphing into something much more heated, something that I've been craving all day, for my entire life it seems.

This month has felt like a hurricane that nearly swept me out to sea, and in the midst of it, I found a treasure, a man with eyes as bright as diamonds named Jasper Wilder.

But somewhere out there is a man named Leo Granger, a man who was once Jasper's best friend, a man who claims to share my strange ability. He says he has the answers I crave, and I wonder if that's true.

Or perhaps more to the point, he's a bounty hunter for some US agency that wants me in a cage for their own use.

If Jasper doesn't trust him, why should I?

As wonderful as things are with Jasper at the moment, as they are in my life in general, I can't help but think this is just the calm before the terrible storm.

Somebody is onto me, and they want answers.

Something tells me they won't rest until they get them.

And I'm fairly certain I won't be safe if they do.

Recipe

Country Cottage Café Apple Walnut Cinnamon Rolls

Hello! It's me, Bizzy Baker. Confession: I burn everything I even think about baking. But the guests of the Country Cottage Inn are crazy about my best friend Emmie's Apple Walnut Cinnamon Rolls. Emmie is in charge of the Country Cottage Café and was blessed with more talent in the kitchen than one person should ever be allowed. Of course, I helped her hone the recipe through trial and error, and lots and lots of taste-testing. It's a tough job but somebody had to do it. And lucky for me, Emmie makes the world's best cinnamon rolls known to man.

Enjoy with a nice glass of milk or coffee.
Warning! These will go fast.

Sweet Dough

1 cup of warm milk (Room temperature, not hot. Preferably whole milk.)

2- ½ teaspoons or ¼ ounce (one package) Active Dry Yeast (preferably rapid rise)

4 tablespoons of granulated sugar

1 teaspoon salt

1 large egg (gently whisked)

1/3 cup butter melted

4 cups all-purpose flour

In a small bowl dissolve yeast into warm milk (about 15 minutes until foamy.)

In a stand mixer bowl, or another larger bowl, combine sugar, salt, egg, butter, and yeast and milk mixture. Combine in a stand mixer with a dough hook.

Slowly add in flour, one cup at a time, at about medium speed until dough forms and pulls away from the sides of the bowl. Dough should be smooth, velvety and soft.

Put the dough in a large bowl coated with cooking spray or butter. Cover with either plastic wrap or a damp towel and let sit in a warm place for 1 hour, until dough has doubled in size.

Punch down the dough and roll into a 20 x 12 rectangle

Cinnamon Filling

3/4 cup brown sugar
3 tablespoons ground cinnamon
1/3 cup melted butter

Apple Walnut Filling

2 small to medium Golden Delicious apples or other apples that are known to be friendly for baking.
1 cup finely chopped walnuts

Peel, core and cut apples into rough slices. Boil until soft (about eight minutes). Mince or mash apples and mix in chopped walnuts.

Brush dough thoroughly with melted butter.

Combine ground cinnamon and brown sugar and sprinkle evenly over the dough.

With a spoon, dollop apple walnut mixture evenly over the dough.

Carefully roll the dough lengthwise, nice and tight. Trim edges and cut the roll into twelve even slices. (About one and a half inches each)

Place in a covered baking dish and let rise an additional 30 minutes (rolls should double in size).

While rolls are busy rising, pre-heat oven to 350°.

Once the rolls finish rising, you are finally ready to bake!

Place the rolls uncovered (either in an oven safe baking dish or a cookie sheet will work fine, too) in the oven for 20-25 minutes or until lightly browned.

Icing

½ cup butter, softened

1/3 cup cream cheese, softened (about 4 oz.)

1 ½ cup powdered sugar

½ teaspoon vanilla extract *Emmie uses 1 teaspoon because she likes the flavor!

2 tablespoons milk

In a medium bowl, mix butter, cream cheese, vanilla and milk, blending it well. Add powdered sugar a half a cup at a time, working it into the mixture until smooth. Pour over fresh baked cinnamon rolls.

Serve warm and enjoy!

Look for **Dog Days of Murder (Country Cottage Mysteries 2)** coming up next!

Thank you for reading **Kittyzen's Arrest (Country Cottage Mysteries 1).** If you enjoyed this book, please consider leaving a review at your point of purchase.

Acknowledgements

Thank you, the reader, for coming along on this amazing journey with us! We hope you love Cider Cove as much as we do. We are SUPER excited to share the next book with you! So much happens and so much changes. Thank you from the bottom of our hearts for taking this wild roller coaster ride with us. We cannot wait to take you on the next leg of the adventure.

Special thank you to the following people for taking care of this book—Kaila Eileen Turingan-Ramos, Kathryn Jacoby, Jodie Tarleton, Lisa Markson, Ashley Marie Daniels and Margaret Lapointe. And a very big shout out to Lou Harper for designing the world's best covers.

A heartfelt thank you to Paige Maroney Smith for being so amazing.

And last, but never least, thank you to Him who sits on the throne. Worthy is the Lamb! Glory and honor and power are yours. We owe you everything, Jesus.

About the Author

Bellamy Bloom

Bellamy Bloom writes cozy mysteries filled with humor, intrigue and a touch of the supernatural. When she's not writing up a murderous storm she's snuggled by the fire with her two precious pooches, chewing down her to-be-read pile and drinking copious amounts of coffee.

Visit her at:

www.authorbellamybloom.com

Addison Moore

Addison Moore is a ***New York Times, USA Today,*** and ***Wall Street Journal*** bestselling author who writes mystery, psychological thrillers and romance. Her work has been featured in ***Cosmopolitan*** Magazine. Previously she worked as a therapist on a locked psychiatric unit for nearly a decade. She resides on the West Coast with her husband, four wonderful children, and two dogs where she eats too much chocolate and stays up way too late.

When she's not writing, she's reading. Addison's Celestra Series has been optioned for film by **20th Century Fox.**

Feel free to visit her at:

www.addisonmoore.com

Made in the USA
Las Vegas, NV
24 December 2024

15321105R00163